BY PINCKNEY BENEDICT

Town Smokes

The Wrecking Yard

THE WRECKING YARD

The

WRECKING

YARD

stories by

PINCKNEY BENEDICT

NAN A. TALESE

DOUBLEDAY

NEW YORK   LONDON   TORONTO   SYDNEY   AUCKLAND

F

F
BEN

PUBLISHED BY DOUBLEDAY

a division of
Bantam Doubleday Dell Publishing Group, Inc.
666 Fifth Avenue, New York, New York 10103

DOUBLEDAY and the portrayal of an anchor
with a dolphin are trademarks of
Doubleday, a division of Bantam Doubleday Dell
Publishing Group, Inc.

Book design by Marysarah Quinn

Material in this collection has been previously published,
in slightly different form, as follows: "Rescuing Moon"
in *Southern Magazine*; "The Electric Girl" and "The Wrecking
Yard" in *The Ontario Review*; "The Panther" in *Wigwag*;
"Getting over Arnette" in *Hot Type*, edited by John Miller
and *Equator* magazine, published by Collier Books.

Library of Congress Cataloging-in-Publication Data
Benedict, Pinckney
The wrecking yard : stories / by Pinckney Benedict. — 1st ed.
          p.   cm.
          I. Title.
       PS3552.E5398W74   1992
813'.54—dc20   91-13004
                                                    CIP

ISBN 0-385-42021-8

10 8 6 4 2 1 3 5 7 9

FIRST EDITION

FOR JOYCE AND RAY

ACKNOWLEDGMENTS

The author wishes to express his thanks to the following for their support during the writing of this book: James A. Michener and the Copernicus Society; the Hill School; Oberlin College; David Black; and Rick Hilton.

CONTENTS

GETTING OVER ARNETTE

Loftus and Bone headed over to the Bowl*O*Drome to take in the women's leagues and see if they could get Loftus's mind off of Arnette. Arnette was the redheaded woman that had run off with some college puke a couple of days before and had broken Loftus's heart and shattered his life.

Loftus had had some time to think events through, but still he couldn't stop running the final bit over in his head. The whole thing took just a minute to consider.

There was Arnette and there was this guy that looked like he was a fast tight end for some state school somewhere and there was skinny sad-sack Loftus standing watching them go off together. Loftus whipped a brick at them from the loose pile outside the cellar door, but that was after the Pontiac was already in motion out of the yard, just too late altogether. The brick hit the trunk of the car and did some damage, but

1

Loftus couldn't find much satisfaction in something a couple of bucks' worth of Bondo was going to be able to fix.

So now Loftus looked at everything around him with a whitened mute expression on his face, behind which that one scene played. It was with him when he stared at the half-dozen spinning ceiling fans of the place and the way they kept the yellow bug-loaded fly strips going in some crazy helical motion from their wind. It just kept on unreeling, even when little Sunny Tatum was on deck for her team doing her stretching exercises and deep knee bends in the shorts she wore to bowl in.

"Watch her go," Bone said and pointed at Alley 17, where she was. You could see just the leg bands of her lemon-colored panties when she was in her squat. Loftus and Bone were sitting at one of the tables behind the lanes. They were the only men in the place, and the women kept looking at them back over their shoulders in a suspicious and uneasy manner. Loftus chewed his underlip.

"Jesus Christ," Bone said. "It was a bad idea from the start and a sorry love affair. You never knew a single person that loved a redheaded woman like her and got away from it with a whole skin. Never happen."

Bone had been wondering what Sunny Tatum looked like naked since they were in high school together. Watching her make her approach to the lane in her shorts and team T-shirt, he guessed he could pretty much figure it out. The Rolling Pins was the name of her team, it said on the back of her shirt. The healthy wholesome bounce and heft of her was like a revelation to Bone.

"It might be you could spend some time in the arms of somebody made like Sunny Tatum and survive it okay," Bone said. "But a woman like that Arnette is all the time going off with somebody," he said.

"I imagine I'm the expert on that one particular issue," Loftus said.

"I expect you are at that," Bone said.

It was mainly a group of nicely cushioned married ladies that belonged to the leagues, which oftentimes encouraged Loftus and tempted him, but tonight there was nothing for him. Grade-school teachers and beauticians and lonely-housewife sherry drunks looked all the same—tired and slack, with no essential grace. He figured Arnette had taken that desirous portion of him with her in the college puke's avocado Catalina.

"I told my future to you at the very beginning of it," Loftus said. "We was sitting over at Tiny's. That's the kind of woman that'll jerk the heart right out of a person's living rib cage, I said. I had my eyes open. I wasn't blind to the danger of it."

Bone nodded. "You did say it. You knew it was bound to occur this way, and still you're hurting anyhow. So I wonder what good is it in a foresight like that."

Down on the lanes, Sunny Tatum left herself a nasty split on the first ball of the frame. She was bowling with one of those colored plastic balls, swirled red and silver in a hazy pattern, with the holes drilled very close together to accommodate her slender grip. Loftus watched the colored ball as it spun strange and lovely down the lane.

When she missed the tough pickup on the split, Sunny stamped her foot on the foul line and made the buzzer go off. She had on little ankle socks with pink pompoms above the heels.

"I'm dead, Bone," Loftus said. He gestured at the eight lanes of women before them. "I thought this would do it for me, but I was wrong. I'm dead and just sitting here waiting for the rot and the worms to start in on me."

"You ain't dead," Bone said. "Just asleep or maybe

stunned a little in your spirit, is all. You'll wake back up to it after a while," he said.

Loftus wasn't listening. He watched Mary Teasdale as she put one right in the 1–3 pocket and dropped all ten pins. She was the dentist's good-looking wife and anchorwoman in the Rolling Pins lineup. A woman that could really put speed on the ball usually got to Loftus one way or another, and Mary Teasdale had an arm on her that was taut with muscle and springy tendon. He couldn't find the interest anywhere inside of him.

"I went out with this girl one time," Bone said, "that was the daughter from a back-road rock-hard Baptist preacher's family and very difficult to get along with. She told me her daddy had give her a sharp old knife and said that she was to feel free to stick it in me if I so much as touched her on her tits or wherever. She showed it to me. Little bitty letter opener is what it really was, but plenty pointed."

"Son of a bitch," Loftus said. "That old man must of been somebody's gift to the world."

"Whether it was the old man give it to her or whether she just took it on herself I never did know," Bone said. "She was a real piece of work, was that one. I took it off of her after we got out of the movies walking home, and she only did manage to get it into me the one time." He pointed to a place on his forearm that could have been made by a BB from a Daisy pump gun or the lead of a pencil point a long time ago. Loftus nodded.

"So I'm bleeding like a pig down my arm and holding that knife and grabbing on to her while she's trying to get away from me back to home. She's gabbling and praying to God to take this cup from her lips or whatever. There we are out in the middle of somebody's empty back field, I don't know whose, the game is all mine, and guess what? After all that hoo-rah, I find out I don't want to touch her anyhow. The thing's just got no intrigue to it anymore."

"What do you know," Loftus said.

"Life's just funny like that sometimes," Bone said. "You never really do know what it is you're after at any given moment in time. Like that Arnette. She thought she was after you and what does it turn out she wants? Not you, that's what. And there for a while you sure thought she was after you too. It's a fact and you got to admit it."

"There it is," Loftus said.

He sat back in his plastic chair and regarded the swaying backsides of the bowling teams. The Pink Ladies looked like they were having a hot night, all women that worked together at the Penney's downtown. The teams around them kept shouting out in shocked despair at their precision and continuing good fortune.

"You all ain't supposed to win," one of the nearby women called to them. The Pink Ladies had been up to then the absolute basement of the league.

"I guess you ain't so much now," one of the Pink Ladies said in the direction of the Rolling Pins. Mary Teasdale and the others ignored her.

"They's a lane open down there if you want to throw a couple of balls," Bone said. "Come on, you'll feel better if you get up and get going. Move around some."

Loftus had cash in his pockets to pay for a couple of games. He got up and started thrusting his fingers into the balls on the alley's racks, looking for one to fit him. "I'll get us some shoes," Bone said.

Loftus found a ball that he could use. It was not one of the colored ones, but just a flat-black ball. He decided that was okay with him, swung the ball on the end of his arm a couple of times to get the feel of it right.

He went on down to the open lane, and Bone came after him with the shoes. "Hey you, Sunny Tatum," Bone said in a loud voice, so that he could be heard over the clash of the pins and the rumble of the balls on the hardwood lanes. They had the lane right next to where the Rolling Pins were.

The team turned to look them over with very little friendliness in their attitude, Mary Teasdale and Sunny Tatum and all, which embarrassed Loftus but which seemed to put a fire under Bone. "Hey," he said again when Sunny was facing him and couldn't ignore that he was talking straight to her.

"Hey back," she said to him in a way that was flirtatious but that Loftus figured meant at the same time You, Bone, want me but won't get to lay a finger on me in this our lifetime. Loftus set his ball down in the return chute, hit the button to make the pin setter lay down their pins. The contact in the button was corroded, and Loftus had to jab at it a couple of times to get the thing to function.

"Looks like you guys ain't doing any too good," Bone said to the Rolling Pins. His tone was easy and his face was a shining invitation to all of them and to Sunny Tatum in specific. He held the ball he had picked out cradled in the crook of his arm like it was a football helmet.

"We're not guys and we aren't doing any too bad either," Mary Teasdale said to him. "So why don't you just bowl your game and get on with it like you ought to be doing. We're in league play here." Bone looked at Sunny Tatum to see what was up with her, but it was her turn to bowl and she was concentrating down the lane.

She released the ball smoothly, followed through with force. Bone noticed a tremor in one of her calves and an answering twitch in her stiffened forearm that he took as a sign of imminent surrender to the force of his personality. The ball slammed the headpin straight on and left her with another of her 7–10 splits, which was her greatest problem in bowling.

"Dammit," Mary Teasdale said to her. It just about made Sunny Tatum cry to be talked to that way, and it just about broke Bone's newly tender heart to watch it happen. The strain of the Pink Ladies' rise from obscurity was beginning to tell on Mary Teasdale and her entire team.

Sunny missed her pickup again, just sailed the ball straight down the lane and between the split pins. "Field goal," one of the Pink Ladies called out, and the rest of the team laughed.

"That's okay, honey girl," Bone said to her. "Everybody's got a down day." He still hadn't set his ball in the chute. Sunny gave him a look that had a little bit of a smile in it.

Loftus polished his ball with a towel that somebody had left behind them at the lane. "Wayne," the black ball had inscribed on it in yellow letters just under the thumbhole. "I'm going to give it a shot now, Bone," Loftus said.

"Why is it you ain't giving me a hand here, good buddy?" Bone said to him. He kept his lips in a grin for the women, but his teeth were clenched together. "This whole entire deal is for your benefit, after all," he said.

"Hey," Loftus said to the women, who weren't looking at him anyhow. He hefted the ball and stepped up to the line. The soles of the bowling shoes were slick, so he watched his footing.

"My friend here not long ago underwent a very bad time is why he's being so unsociable," Bone said to the women. Mary Teasdale looked like she was ready to spit but ignored him as best she could. "Affair of the heart," Bone said, pressing his hands flat against his chest. He had to put his ball down to make the gesture.

"Some gal busted him, did she?" Sunny Tatum said. She had sharp white even-spaced teeth and a voice like cotton candy.

Loftus rolled a gutter ball, and when it came back to him in the ball return he rolled another one. "Your go," he said to Bone. He didn't care about the gutter balls. He didn't even mark them down on the score sheet. Scoring bowling was something confusing that he wasn't sure he remembered right.

"Tore him all up one side and down the other," Bone said to Sunny Tatum. "Used him for what he's worth and then left with somebody bigger and stronger and better-looking. He's not hardly a man anymore after he got his heart eat out like that, and I'm just here trying to help him get over it."

"Bowling help a man cure his love thing?" Sunny said.

"It ain't like that, Arnette and me," Loftus said to Bone. To the women in the bowling alley he said, "For a time it was as good as good, until it went bad." They just looked at him.

"The attractive presence of such ladies as yourselves is starting to have a redeeming effect on him already, I imagine," Bone said.

The Rolling Pins, all except for Sunny Tatum, had by this time had enough of Bone and of Loftus by implication and association, and Mary Teasdale went after the manager of the place to get the problem taken care of. She didn't even threaten Bone, she was so serious in her determination. She just went. Some women in a couple of the other teams cheered her as she steamed off.

"It'll teach them to strip us naked with their eyes," one big lady said to her friend.

The friend crossed her arms over her bosom. "That ain't all they was doing with their eyes," she said. "Poking and prodding like that, it's a sin," she said under her breath.

Only the Pink Ladies cared for the presence of Bone and Loftus at all, and that was because they figured the men as potential good-luck charms. Also they had noted the distress the men were causing among the other teams, and they applauded that.

"I ain't telling nobody to leave," the manager said to Mary Teasdale when she complained to him. "I'm taking exactly nobody off them lanes." He was a little gray old man that sat on a stool in a storage closet behind some wire mesh. He handed out shoes and scorecards through a slot in the mesh and always took one shoe of the bowler's as security, even when it was somebody like Mary Teasdale, who came to the place every week practically and who plainly wouldn't walk off with the alley's greasy Lysol-smelling footwear. He had a cut-down baseball bat that he kept back in there with him, and he swore he would use it when the occasion arose. Other times he kept to himself and minded his own business.

"You want to get them out of here, that's you," the old man said. Mary Teasdale clutched at the wire near his face. "Me, I seen nothing thus far calls for that sort of handling."

"We'll make them leave," Mary Teasdale said. She was puffed like a toad with anger and poisonous emotion. "We don't have to put up with that kind of thing in here. Not by a long sight do we have to."

"That's you," the old man said, but he was talking to Mary Teasdale's back as she headed for her lane. The other women saw her returning with her complaint, which was their common complaint, unredressed, and they came together into a sudden single monumental resolve. It passed like a swift weather-bearing wind among them. They set down their bowling balls and squared their shoulders and moved in around Loftus and Bone.

Loftus looked at the stony faces of the women all around him. Bone was caught up in Sunny Tatum, who didn't seem to mind his attention and was not part of the general wave of resentment. Loftus tapped him on the back. "Bone," he said very softly. "Oh, Bone."

"Lord, Lord," one of the Pink Ladies said. Her voice was loud and the only noise in the alley, since all the bowling had recently and abruptly ceased. "Them boys had better get their ass in gear."

"What is it that you need from me exactly?" Bone said to Loftus. Then Mary Teasdale moved into his field of vision in anger and fury and he knew something was up. She took hold of his forearms and another woman grabbed him at his waist and there were hands in Loftus's hair and twisted in his clothing. Someone jabbed a sharp elbow into his side and he felt the press of bodies against him. He was held roughly up and could not fall.

"You need a lesson," Mary Teasdale called into Bone's ear. He jerked back but couldn't slip the grasp of a dozen hands. "You need to learn how to be like gentlemen," Mary Teasdale shouted at Loftus.

The women bowlers leaned hard against the men. They pushed them and shoved them and it was a painful progress, but Loftus and Bone did not cry out as the women took them in hand and forced them to the glass doors of the place and through and on out into the dark.

. . .

"Hey, men," Eugene said to Loftus and Bone. Eugene owned and operated Tiny's, which was a saloon and pool and pinball place in town.

"Beer," Bone said to Eugene, climbing up onto a stool and pointing in front of him. Bone was smoldering like a fire that you have pissed on but not adequately.

"Me too," Loftus said. He shook his head, looking at Bone and wanting to laugh. It made him feel nervous and crazy, left by Arnette and then beat up by women and thinking it was a pretty hilarious juncture in his life. Bone hung his head down near the bar and swallowed without enjoying at all.

"You men don't look so good," Eugene said. "Always into something wicked, ain't you."

Bone turned on his stool and looked out over the bar, which was quiet and empty except for one guy at a table near the back. "Who is it back there?" Bone said to Eugene. The guy at the table was somebody that he didn't know, and that was unusual in Tiny's.

Eugene leaned close. "That there," he said, "is a bona fide former member of the United States Armed Forces that fought in their secret war in Vietnam, Republic of. At least that's what he says he is."

"Secret war," Bone said. "What secret war is it that he means?"

"I ast him that," Eugene said. "The one they tried to kill all the niggers with and the other undesirables, he said. Damn near worked, too, to hear him claim it. He gets all heated up over it if you talk to him. It's a subject you might want to steer clear of."

"Is he a nigger?" Bone said.

"Don't think so," Eugene said.

Loftus and Bone and Eugene looked at the guy just sitting back there sucking on the ice cubes of his drink, and he looked at them sitting where they were. He sucked an ice cube into his mouth and crushed it with a loud noise and swallowed. Then he did the same again.

"What is he staring at like that?" Bone said.

"Leave him be," Loftus said.

The guy pointed at their feet. "I am told that what you have there is a style of dress favored on many of the nation's better university campuses," he said. Loftus and Bone still had on the bowling shoes that they'd been wearing when they were ejected from the Bowl·O·Drome.

Loftus regretted the loss of his Durango steel-toed boots more than almost anything else about the evening. Bone had grabbed up the one sneaker he'd been allowed by the old man to take to the lane, but it had been torn from him and carried off as a prize by some woman in a Pin Smashers shirt.

"But you don't neither of you look like something that might be going to college right away, do you," the guy said. Neither Loftus nor Bone said anything.

After a time the guy spread his arms wide and said, "And for your unique footwear, all this have I rendered unto you." He was looking just at Bone now, having singled him out to speak to. "So come unto me and receive it," the guy said. He was gesturing all around at the walls and chairs of the place and the liquor bottles behind the bar. He dumped a little of the ice over the edge of his glass.

"The hell you say," Bone said to him. "This here's Eugene's place. It says Tiny's outside on the sign, but it belongs to this fellow Eugene all right."

Eugene gestured at him to be left out of it.

"I don't mean just the bar," the guy said. "I'm talking about everything. The whole shooting match. The entire United States of America and the free world that tags along with it. That's what I'm talking about."

"And you give all that to me," Bone said. "I thank you for that," he said, and he laughed.

"Hell," the guy said. "I don't know if I would of done it if it had just been this little bar in this one little town. That might not of been worth it. But it was everything and so I killed and died for it and just about everybody I know killed and died for it."

"Well, sure," Loftus said. "I imagine we could set you up a drink through Eugene if you want," he said.

"I'd take a drink," the guy said. "I'd take a drink to the end of the world, and have," he said. "You come over here and drink with me and tell me what is here to recommend itself in this tired town." He pushed out one of the other chairs at his table with his foot as an invitation. He had on a pair of black thick-soled jump boots.

Bone went and sat with the guy, so Loftus followed him. The guy's name it turned out was Leonard Meadows, and he was a big old boy from a town out in the desert of West Texas called Mankinville. "Even sorrier and littler than this place is, if you can think of such a thing," he said.

Leonard Meadows had come up to work in the slaughter plant that was over near the railroad tracks, and he knew a great deal about various cuts and varieties of meat. He was making pretty good money there and took to paying for the drinks after a time, which was good as Loftus's finances were quickly getting strapped and Bone never carried any money with him if he could help it, even when he had any.

"I worked over to that plant one summer back a few years ago," Loftus said. "Man, I don't remember so much about it except that it was nasty and greasy hard work and smelled just about worse than anything since. How is it you can stand it all the time?"

"I been worse places and done worse things than that, I am here to relay to you," Leonard Meadows said. "That there's a picnic is what it is." It was then that Bone and Loftus remembered about him being in Vietnam, and they figured that was what he was talking about and felt bad for making him recall something like that. But when they apologized he told them not to worry.

He told them a mess of stories that had to do with assault rifles and rice paddies and helicopter dust-offs and long-range patrols. He mentioned stuff like phosphorus rounds and grenade launchers and flamethrowers as if they were normal parts of the world and just sitting around there in the room to be touched and handled and used on an everyday basis.

He talked to Loftus and Bone about guys that he had managed to kill successfully and about guys that had killed him only a little bit less successfully, and sometimes he knew the names of those guys or had found them out or just made them up. He talked about Arvin, which he seemed to bitterly detest, and Brother Charles, for whom he seemed to have a sorrowful sort of respect, and a city by the name of Hue where he and some of his buddies had got into hardship.

"One guy I knew," Leonard Meadows said, "got jobbed with a punji stick and ended up with a hole about the size of a pencil in his leg. That thing dribbled and bled for the longest time, and it never did close up. Something Charles did to the stick, poisoned it or puked on it or shit on it most likely. The guy that was stuck swore it was Ho himself shit on that stick, the infection was so evil and bad-smelling. They took him to Japan and everwhere with all the clean smart doctors trying to get that leg to heal but it never did."

"Jesus," Loftus said.

"Just another example of what the wily Southeast Asian can get himself up to when you come into his area, buddy," Leonard Meadows said. He finished with his drink and gestured to Eugene to bring him another one.

"I got to shut it down soon," Eugene said. "Wife," he said.

"You bet, sport," Leonard said. "You look like the kind of folks that can find some trouble when you want," he said to Loftus and Bone. "So tell me about the wars you boys been fighting recently."

"We seen some trouble all right," Loftus said. "It was a bunch of women that didn't care for us so much."

"Lady-killers such as yourselves," Leonard said. "I find it hard to imagine."

"Well, him there," Bone said, pointing at Loftus, "he had this woman and she walked out on him was the start of it. Arnette. Turns out she's been stepping out on the town and it might even of been more than just one man. And he's all wore out because she's redheaded and good-looking and very stuck on herself in reality and if the truth be told." Bone glared at Loftus. "That's where the trouble lays," he said.

"Redheaded local girl name of Arnette and hot to look at," Leonard Meadows said, and he scratched at his head as if he was considering his past. "Sure, I do believe I've screwed her a time or two myself," he said.

Loftus knew it was probably just a joke, but he grabbed Leonard Meadows's shirt collar anyway and started to drag him across the tabletop. He made the move before he knew what to do about it or considered the depth of trouble that would result. A wide piece of Leonard's shirt came away in his hand.

He never did see Leonard Meadows hit him or what he hit him with, but he did see Bone go for the knife he carried clipped in an ankle sheath. He was lying on the floor and couldn't find a way to tell Bone not to do it. Leonard Meadows kicked Bone in the face with one of those big jump boots and shattered his jaw. Bone gave it up and lay down and bled on the board floor of the place. He spat a couple of times and then held his tongue out of his mouth. There were teeth on his tongue and they fell off and made a little clattering sound on the floor.

Eugene stepped out from behind the bar but stopped when Leonard Meadows turned and faced him. Leonard was standing in a strange way, erect but somehow curled like a snake ready to strike. Eugene figured he knew karate or some other kind of tricks that they teach in the military.

Leonard extended his right arm. "Do you crave to see your pancreas laying here in the palm of my hand?" he said to Eugene.

"No sir," Eugene said. "I got enough problems on my own already."

"I imagine you do," Leonard Meadows said. He looked around the room like he was sorry to have done what he had to do there, and then he walked out.

Loftus reached a hand up to his head, afraid of what he might find. He was amazed when he learned that he couldn't really feel his head at all. He wondered if it was his skull or his hand that had something wrong with it, and what was it that could be wrong would make him feel like that. He closed his eyes so he wouldn't have to look at Bone lying down there next to him.

Eugene kneeled down by the two of them. "Oh my Lord in heaven," he said. Loftus didn't know which one of them he was worried about or whether it was both of them in dire trouble and need of a blessing. He kept his eyes closed and drifted away from the scene as best he was able, passing after a time into unconsciousness.

Loftus was not overly shocked when Arnette came back home alone into his arms and affections shortly after the fight. The college puke didn't even bring her back but made her take the bus for nearly five hours to get home, and she was in a sore mood and tired from the dust and the heat and carrying her suitcase.

Loftus was still wearing a patch on his head, but the stitches were coming out soon and that was good because the whole thing had started to itch like a son of a gun.

"You heard I got busted up, hey," Loftus said to her. She looked at him like she was surprised from where she was unpacking her case in the bedroom.

"No," she said. "I never heard a single thing about it." She shoved some more underwear in a drawer.

"I'm sorry it happened to you," she said. "Glad you didn't get your teeth kicked out like old Bone," she said when he told her the rest about the fight.

"I'm happy to have you back here with me," he said to her.

"You bet you are," she said.

He never asked her about Leonard Meadows or what he had said, because he was pretty certain it had been a joke and he didn't like to think about that evening if he could help it. Bone had told him that he knew Leonard was now living out on the Ridge Road in Sunny Tatum's trailer with Sunny Tatum. She had taken him in out of love and affection to help cure his war injuries which were psychological and mental and difficult for him to deal with on his own.

"His injuries," Bone said through his wired jaw. "We ought to go after him. Get a gun and just go nail the son of a bitch."

Loftus hated to think of what might happen to them if they went out against Leonard with something so serious as a gun. Drinking soup and milkshakes and being silent most of the day, Bone had taken a grim turn somewhere inside of himself.

When Loftus finally did ask Arnette what it was that made her come back to him, she told him that it had just been a sex thing with that college guy and never serious at all. Loftus nodded at her like he understood and it was okay and acknowledged to himself that if he had been given a chance at a sex thing he might have taken it up in the same way.

"Don't ever do like that again," he said to Arnette one night when he got drunk and bold enough and the love he had for her welled up strong inside of his breast. "It like to killed me when you went," he said. There were tears in his eyes.

"No promises, you know that," Arnette said to him. Her eyes were blue and bright and her red hair framed her face. "Can't you just be happy with what it is that we have? That is one thing I learned from my time away, if not a single thing else, that you got to seize the day." She touched him on his bald stitched patch and smiled.

"All right," Loftus said. "I put no conditions on you." And he was happy in the saying of it and proud to live in that fashion, even though he knew that for his suffering she would never leave him for another man again.

THE WRECKING YARD

When Mr. Papaduke drives into the salvage yard with the '66 Impala on the flatbed, Perry decides that the time has come to trade vehicles. Perry runs the crusher at Papaduke's Auto Salvage and Wrecking Yard in Maxwell. He owns an old Willys jeep that his father gave him, and it's getting hard to find parts for the thing. Mr. Papaduke parks the truck in front of his one-room cinder-block office, and Perry hoists himself up onto the bed to check the car out.

"Come down off of there," Mr. Papaduke says to Perry as he gets out of the truck. He's a tall gaunt old man with a narrow nose and white bushy eyebrows. He's missing the two smallest fingers off his left hand, from a time when the jack slipped out from under a pickup truck he was working on.

Perry climbs down from the back of the truck, and Mr. Papaduke leans into the cab and pulls the lever that tilts the flatbed so they can roll the car off it. Perry's already picturing himself in the long low white Chevrolet, cruising across the big levels. The car has the original hubcaps all the way around, with the little embossed Chevy symbol on the spinner.

"Does it run?" he asks as the flatbed's winch pays out cable and the Impala rolls down the incline.

"Sure it runs," Mr. Papaduke says. "That's what got it in trouble."

"What'd you pay for it?" Weasel wants to know as he comes up to inspect the Impala. Weasel works part-time at the yard, stripping the salvageable speed equipment off the wrecked cars for Mr. Papaduke before Perry puts them through the crusher. He's small and wiry, with thin lips and eyes so pale a blue they're almost white.

"Paid nothing for it," Mr. Papaduke says.

"Nothing," Perry says. The car is on the ground now, and Perry ducks under the front bumper to unhook the winch. While he's down there, he checks what he can see of the frame, the suspension. Not so bad. There's still a good bit of tread on the tires. He wonders what is wrong with it to make it a free car.

"Hell," Mr. Papaduke says, "the woman that called me wanted to get rid of it so bad she didn't think to ask for a dime. Ended up I talked her into paying a fifteen-dollar towing fee."

"No shit," Weasel says, and shakes his head in admiration. He is a freak about funny cars and has no real use for the stock Impala, but Mr. Papaduke's business sense impresses him.

"We'll get the chrome breather out of that Shelby Mustang, and the headers," he tells Mr. Papaduke. The Mustang came into the yard a couple of days ago. It got rear-ended by a highballing log truck, but most of the front end is still recoverable. "Probably them high-compression heads too," he says.

"Do it," Mr. Papaduke says, and Weasel heads into the back part of the yard. He's been swiping performance parts for a 1970 GTO he's rebuilding, and Mr. Papaduke knows about it. He's told Perry that he lets Weasel get away with it because stealing keeps Weasel enthusiastic about his job, and Weasel is good at what he does.

Perry crawls out from under the Impala's front end, wipes his hands on his coveralls. "I'll buy it off you," he says. Mr. Papaduke just looks at him, and Perry thinks he might not have heard. "The Impala," he says. "What do you want for it? I'll trade you my Willys on it."

"No," Mr. Papaduke says. He levels the flatbed and coils the cable back on the winch. "You don't want that thing. Can't let you have it anyway."

"It looks like a good car," Perry says. "Why not?" He opens the door of the Impala, sits on the driver's side of the bench front seat. The springs there have gone soft, and he bounces himself against the seat, testing the give. He taps the horn, but there is no sound.

"A guy died in that car," Mr. Papaduke says.

Perry depresses the accelerator, twists the key, and the Impala grinds to life. He gestures out the window at the dozens of ruined cars around them. "Guys died in almost every car we got," he says.

"This one killed himself," Mr. Papaduke says. "He put the car in the garage, then sealed up the garage windows and door-frames with duct tape. He sat and listened to a rock station on the radio and just let the car run and run."

"Suffocated himself," Perry says.

"Carbon monoxide poison," Mr. Papaduke says. "Filled the house with the stuff. Almost got the rest of his family at the same time. His old lady was pretty pissed about that."

"He gassed his wife?"

"Not his wife," Mr. Papaduke says. "His mother. He wasn't any more than about eighteen years old. His father passed out cold before they figured out what was happening."

Perry turns the Impala off. The engine diesels for a second, hiccuping and rolling, before it stops. "And she gave you money to haul the car off."

Mr. Papaduke grins. "Sure she did," he says. "I told her I'd squash it flat for her. She's still got a headache and a ringing in her ears from the exhaust. She sees spots before her eyes and can't tell if she's ever going to be all right again."

"Did he mean to do that?" Perry asks. "Did he want to take the whole family with him?"

"I asked the mother that," Mr. Papaduke says. "She says no. She says he was just a fuck-up."

"I give old Papaduke five parts, I take one," Weasel says. "I give him another five parts, I take one. It's perfect." He's sitting in the passenger seat of the yard's big Fruehauf, the wrecker they use to pull semi tractors.

Perry and Weasel are on their way to some kind of truck smash on Droop Pike, up on the side of Big Lime Mountain. They heard about it on the Bearcat scanner at Papaduke's. Since the yard is right at the base of Big Lime, they decided to check it out. Perry drives.

Some guy is on the CB jabbering about the accident. He's at the scene, apparently. "They're all over the place," he says. "Oh Jesus, oh Jesus."

Weasel picks up the mike. "Clear the channel, please," he says.

The guy keeps on. He's weeping into the radio about legs and bones and hair. "Clear the channel," Weasel says. Still the weeping.

"This guy," Weasel says. He hangs the mike on its hook, turns the volume down.

"I got a nitrous injection system out of that Shelby 'stang the other day," he says. "I give him headers and shifters and all, and I don't tell him about the nitrous so he never misses it. I'll get six hundred horsepower out of the GTO with that nitrous oxide."

Perry shifts down as they climb a switchback that's banked the wrong way. He's keeping his eyes peeled for the wreck. "Mr. Papaduke knows you steal stuff, Weasel," he says.

"Bullshit," Weasel says. He licks his lips. "He does?"

Perry pulls the Fruehauf over onto the narrow shoulder, sets the flashers going. A truck, a big beef hauler, has gone through the guardrail of a sharp curve on the highway's downhill lane. The truck lies on its side on the slope below the road. The slotted walls of the livestock trailer are buckled. Perry and Weasel have beaten the cops and the emergency types to the scene.

Perry climbs out of the Fruehauf. He leaves the truck running. The raincaps on the Fruehauf's dual exhaust stacks rattle. "Hey," he says. "Anybody hurt?"

A couple of men are sitting on the twisted guardrail. One of them has his arms wrapped around himself. He's rocking back and forth, sucking his breath painfully between his teeth.

The other man stands to greet Perry. "Just Matthew here," he says. "A little."

He's wearing a cap with the beef company's name on it.

"XL Meats," it says, under a little picture of a cow jumping over the moon. "It's the undertakers," he says to Matthew.

There's a terrible roaring and bawling coming up to them from the scrub and brush around the wrecked beef hauler. Perry lights a couple of emergency flares and tosses them behind the Fruehauf and in front of it. They give off a greasy smoke, and their orange flame is pale in the sunlight.

Weasel has trotted up the hill another dozen yards to a little yellow Datsun that's parked there. "Get off that thing," he shouts, tapping the driver's window with his fist. The man inside has a CB mike to his mouth. Tears run down his face.

"This guy's still on the radio," Weasel says, and he waggles the whip antenna on the roof like he's going to snap it. "He won't get off."

"We lost the brakes," the meat company driver says. "Didn't know how long this grade was and just burned them up."

"It happens," Perry says. Hereford steers drift among the trees along the highway, wagging their long heads, dripping foam and blood. A number of them are stretched out on the slope, already dead. As Perry watches, another steer drags itself from the livestock box. Its eyes are white and wild, and it walks with a crippled, limping gait. It heads toward the road and the men. It snorts and woofs.

"Here comes one," Weasel says. He has joined the group at the break in the guardrail. He points at the approaching steer, which whirls and lopes down the hill away from them, careening off the trunks of trees as it goes.

"I think I got busted ribs, Hoover," Matthew says. He tightens his grip on himself, shivers. "I think maybe I popped a lung." Hoover is the uninjured truck driver.

"Spit into your hand," Hoover says. Matthew holds out

his hand, spits into the palm, shows it to Hoover. "No," Hoover says. "If a lung was involved, your spit'd be all shot through with blood."

"Oh," Matthew says. He wipes his hand on the grass at the edge of the road and wraps his arms around himself again.

"So there's nobody else down there," Perry says.

"No," Hoover says. "It was just us." He points up the road at the Datsun. "And that guy. He was riding pretty close behind us. I think it shook him up a little. He won't get out of his car."

"You should hear him on the radio," Weasel says.

Perry moves down the slope to the hauler. He leans back to keep his balance. The truck tore up the ground as it went, snapping off saplings and scrub trees. The broken trunks are splintered and sharp as stakes. Perry moves carefully.

The steers jostle one another and bellow as he passes them, but mostly they are too maimed and shaken up to run away. They do not sound like any cattle that Perry has heard before. The noise they make is hollow, and it caroms off the limestone outcroppings around them, making the stone ring. The smells of manure and shattered flesh mix with the scent of spilled diesel fuel.

"No smoking," Weasel calls down, and he and Hoover laugh. They talk together a minute, and Perry hears Hoover say "barbecue."

The trailer is a total loss, Perry sees, and the tractor too. It is a hoary old International Transtar, heeled over against the oak tree that stopped its slide. The engine block has pulled free of its mountings and protrudes through the grille; one of the fuel tanks has split down its length. The company's jumping-cow logo is painted on the door of the truck cab.

He peers into the livestock box, but there is nothing moving in there, nothing left alive. The steers were hurled against the front bulkhead when the truck slammed to a stop, and many of them are still piled there, legs jutting out at odd angles. In the confusion of bodies it is impossible to tell one animal from another. He touches one of the trailer's tires. The wheel is frozen on its ruined axle.

"You. Come back up here," someone yells. Perry looks, sees that there is a state trooper standing at the edge of the highway. The trooper motions for Perry to come to him. Perry climbs the hill.

"Stay up out of there," the trooper says to Perry. He's a middle-aged man with muscular arms and a solid neck. He has rearranged Perry's flares, moved them farther up the road, and added a few of his own. His hand rests against the butt of his service revolver. His partner is talking to the driver of the Datsun, who has rolled his window down. "That's an accident scene," the trooper says.

"Sure," Perry says. "I've seen accidents before. I drive a wrecker." He points to the idling Fruehauf. The police cruiser is parked immediately behind it. "See? This is nothing new," he says.

The trooper pokes a thick finger into Perry's chest. "Listen, wrecker man," he says. Perry takes a step back to get away from the finger, but the trooper plants it in his breastbone again, painfully. "That comes after," the trooper says. "That's your time, after. This is our time. You get back until we're done with our time."

Perry and the trooper stand face to face for a moment. The two beef company drivers are watching, as is Weasel. Their faces are bland.

"We'll let you know," the trooper says. He turns from Perry and addresses Matthew. "Were you driving?" he says.

"No," Matthew says.

Hoover touches Perry's sleeve. "Any way to get the tractor back on the road again?" He looks worried.

"We'll be lucky to get it up the grade and back to the yard without tearing it apart," Perry says.

"It's a total loss, then," Hoover says.

"Man, you're lucky to be alive," Weasel says.

"Do you mind if I get a second with you, driver?" the trooper says. He takes Hoover's elbow and steers him to a spot a little away from the others.

The trooper's partner, a young man, very trim in his blue uniform, comes down the road toward them. He has apparently finished questioning the driver of the Datsun, and the yellow car pulls onto the road. It does not continue downhill. Instead, it reverses direction and heads back the way it came.

"I believe he was still crying," Weasel says.

As the young trooper approaches Perry and the others, a passing Volkswagen minibus slows and its occupants stare at the torn guardrail. The young trooper motions for them to keep going, and the VW disappears around the next bend.

"I can't stand that noise," the young trooper says. "All the moaning, those cattle. It sounds like a slaughterhouse down there."

The older trooper says, "What do you want to do, Lou?"

"I want to shoot them," the young trooper says. "I want to put those cows out of their misery."

"Steers," Hoover says. The trooper still has him by the elbow. "They're market steers."

"Okay, Lou," the older trooper says. "I've got some questioning to finish up here. You go ahead."

Lou vaults over the guardrail and trots down the hillside. He's quite athletic, moves like an acrobat. He comes to the first of the steers in just a few seconds and draws his sidearm.

"He can't do that," Hoover says.

"You tell him," the older trooper says.

Hoover doesn't move, and Lou puts his service revolver against the side of the floundering steer's head, pulls the trigger. The discharge echoes off the side of Big Lime, and the steers that are still on their feet vanish among the trees. The men can hear them groaning as they move off. Lou's steer continues to thrash for a few moments, and then it subsides.

"I believe he can," the older trooper says and shakes his head. Revolver drawn, Lou pursues the steers down the slope.

"Come on, Weasel," Perry says.

"What did you call him?" the older trooper asks.

"Weasel," Perry says. "It's his name."

The trooper examines Weasel, who grins nervously. "How did you hear about this accident, anyway?" the trooper asks.

"Scanner," Weasel says.

Perry crosses the road, gets into the Fruehauf. The CB is muttering, a weak patter of words under the growl of the wrecker's engine, so Perry turns the sound back up.

"It was awful," a voice says. It is the man Perry and Weasel heard on the way to the accident, the driver of the Datsun.

"Legs and heads and oh, the animals. Dear God, what a sight!" His signal begins to break up as he moves away on the narrow winding road. "Death on such a scale," he says, and then he is gone and there is only static on the radio. Perry turns it off entirely.

The passenger-side door opens and Weasel slides into his seat. His pale eyes are narrow. He slumps in the seat, puts his boots on the dashboard. "He called us vultures," he says.

"Who did?" Perry asks.

"The cop, the beefy one. He says we're parasites on accidents. We swarm around the place where the blood collects, he says."

"Hard to argue," Perry says.

They sit for a while. At the side of the road, the trooper is still questioning Hoover. A Dwyer County ambulance pulls up, and the medical technicians swarm around Matthew. They lay him out on a stretcher and try to examine him, but he refuses to take his arms from around himself. Every couple of minutes Lou's revolver goes off over the rim of the hill. The sound of the shots is muffled by the thick glass of the wrecker's cab.

"That Hoover," Weasel says finally. "What a wheeler-dealer." He is trying hard not to giggle.

"How's that?" Perry says.

"He was trying to sell me beef while you were down at the hauler. He said he knew he had to move the meat quick before it went bad. We're watching them steers stumble around down there and he's trying to get me to buy them, sixty bucks a head. He'd of come down a good deal more if I'd had time to jew him a little. I could of got the whole truckload for three hundred."

"It's July," Perry says. "That stuff will be flyblown before you could do anything with it. It'll be stinking by nightfall."

"I know that," Weasel says. He sounds a little insulted. "That's why I didn't bite. It was just fun listening to him talk."

The ambulance is pulling away, and the trooper has closed his notebook, as if he's done talking to Hoover. The two of them cross the road and Hoover gets into the cruiser.

"Perry?" Weasel says. "Were you kidding, what you said earlier?" He sounds worried.

"Kidding about what?"

"Old man Papaduke. Does he really know I'm ripping him off?"

Before Perry can answer, the trooper is standing on the tow truck's running board, knocking at the window, and it is finally their turn with the wrecked livestock hauler.

"Now we'll see what you're made of," the trooper says.

He stands on the brow of the hill, his eyes shaded by the brim of his round hat, and he watches Perry climb back down to the truck with the winch cable. While the reports of his partner's revolver echo and re-echo from the woods, he stands there like he has all the time in the world, like he really wants to see if they can get the beef hauler back up the slope in one piece.

"One time," Mr. Papaduke tells Perry and Weasel, "I popped the door on this new-model Pontiac with a pry bar. The frame of the car was bent and the door was jammed shut. When I get the door open, all this black water gushes out, all over my legs and shoes. And it's got fish in it. These dead carp plop onto my feet. I screamed like a woman."

It develops that a couple of kids rolled the car into one of the old C & O canals and couldn't get free when the car filled with water. The interior of the car carried a thick coating of noisome bottom silt. Mr. Papaduke's nose wrinkles as he remembers it.

"Were the kids in there?" Weasel asks.

"No," Mr. Papaduke says. "The cops got them out and then called me to get the car. But there were squirrels in there. Two squirrels."

"Squirrels?"

"Yeah," Mr. Papaduke says. "I couldn't figure it. I scooped them out of there with a little camp shovel. A really big squirrel and a little one. So I've got these two drowned mud-covered squirrels, but they're in—" He pauses. "They're in very lifelike poses. Standing up and everything."

"They were stuffed," Perry offers.

"Sure they were," Mr. Papaduke says. "But it baffled the hell out of me for a while. The kids must of had them on the rear deck of the car or something."

"So did you keep them?" Weasel asks.

"No," Mr. Papaduke says. "I had to throw them out. They stank so bad you didn't really want to get close to them. They soaked up a lot of that canal water while they were down there." He takes a bite out of his sandwich. It is lunch break.

"I never ran across anything much in the cars that I went through," Weasel says. "Although I heard about one man that found a glass eye."

"I got a necklace," Perry says. "Little gold chain all wrapped around the gearshift in this Ford Falcon."

"It was a shame to throw them fellows out, too," Mr. Papaduke says. He hasn't been listening. "They looked like they might of been pretty nice squirrels before they got ruined."

Perry can see the Impala from where he sits in the cab of the crane. He has painted it candy-apple red. Mr. Papaduke sold it to him for ninety-nine dollars and the trade of his Willys, on the condition that he would paint it some color other than white and that he would lie to everyone about where he got it from.

"I give that woman a promise," Mr. Papaduke said. "What would she do if she knew that some stranger was riding around in her dead son's car?"

The white paint still shows through the red finish, and Perry decides that he'll go over the car again as soon as he quits work. Mr. Papaduke has the flatbed out on a call, so Perry is alone at the yard. There's a big old sedan yet to run through the crusher, a bulbous rusted Hudson Terraplane that's finally given up the ghost, and then he's done for the day.

He drops the crane's heavy electromagnet onto the roof of the Hudson, picks the car up, drops it into the crushing bay. He smiles and descends from the crane's cab to fire up the hydraulic press. He cups his hands over his ears to drown out the noise while the heavy steel car is being flattened.

When it's done, Perry lifts the Hudson out of the crusher with the crane and adds it to one of the stacks of squashed cars. Inside the ten-foot metal fence around Papaduke's there are maybe a thousand cars in all. Perry has put most of them through the crusher, and they're piled all around the yard. Some of the stacks are twenty, twenty-five feet tall. They make cool dark alleys and blind corridors where he sometimes likes to eat his lunch, with the smell of all that oxidizing metal in his nostrils.

Mr. Papaduke comes back to the yard just as Perry is taping over the windows of the Impala, to keep the paint from them. The remains of an old Barracuda are chained down on the flatbed. The frame of the car is badly distorted. The hood hangs from a single warped hinge. The passenger door sits propped in the back seat, along with the front and rear bumpers and the mashed hoodscoop from a big Weiand blower. Written on the driver's door in looping white script are the words "Hunka Hunka Burnin Love."

"Whose 'cuda?" Perry asks Mr. Papaduke.

"Why?" Mr. Papaduke says. "You want to buy this one too?" He heads on into his office.

The Barracuda has a convertible roof. The light frame of the ragtop is twisted back against the trunk of the car, and the thick roof material hangs from it like a shredded flag.

Perry follows Mr. Papaduke into the office. The walls of the room are covered with hubcaps. Nash, Hudson, Buick, in no kind of order. More hubcaps spill from a careless pile in one corner.

The concrete floor is lined with salvaged equipment: large-faced Sun tachometers, oil temperature meters, pressure gauges, headers and Thrush sidepipes and glasspack mufflers. There is a shifter with a knob shaped to look just like a human hand. Perry doesn't like the idea of getting a vinyl-covered handshake from the thing every time he switches gears.

A narrow path leads through all the stuff to the desk where Mr. Papaduke sits. It is cool in there, and dark. The single window is covered by hanging hubcaps. He has not turned on a light, but just sits there. He is looking toward the door, but Perry is not sure Mr. Papaduke sees him.

"Whose car is that?" Perry says. He jerks a thumb over his shoulder toward the Barracuda. The flatbed is framed in the doorway, but the sunlight glinting on what's left of the Barracuda's sharp silver finish makes it hard to look at. "I don't recognize it."

"Nobody I know," Mr. Papaduke says. "Some idiot. He's room temperature now."

"Elvis fan, I guess," Perry says. "Personally, I never thought much of that fat boy. He could sing a little, but I never knew what it was made him so special."

"He wasn't always fat," Mr. Papaduke says. "I remember him on the TV when he was skinny as a rail." Mr. Papaduke clasps his hands against his own narrow belly.

"I guess," Perry says. "Hey, I bet Weasel will be pissed not to get his hands on that blower. It's trashed."

"Yeah," Mr. Papaduke says. "That's one piece of hurry-up the Weasel won't walk away with."

"Reason I wondered who the car belonged to," Perry says, "is you seemed a little anxious when you came in just now. Glum. I thought maybe you ran across somebody that you knew."

"The car went off a bluff up on Savory Knob," Mr. Papaduke says. "It spun over and over and come down on its top."

"Ouch," Perry says. He knows that the ones where the car turns turtle are always the worst.

"There was a girl in the car with him, apparently. They looked, but they never found her while I was up there."

"Where'd she go?"

"They figure she got pitched out through the roof by the torque. They figure she's hung up in the trees on the cliff face somewhere. There's a search going on up there if you feel like you want to go."

"Maybe," Perry says. "I don't know what I could do for her."

"It was a pretty easy salvage," Mr. Papaduke says. "There was a fire road at the base of the bluff, and the car landed there. I just hooked it up and ran it onto the flatbed with the winch. No sweat."

"That's good, then," Perry says. "That's something."

"Sure," Mr. Papaduke says. He switches on his desk lamp, pulls out the yard's big checkbook and a stack of bills that he's got to pay. He flips open the checkbook, begins to write. "It's something," he says.

Perry sees Weasel's GTO first thing when he gets up to the search site on Savory Knob. Perry's Impala is rattling and pinging as it labors up the knob, and he's afraid that it's going to suck a valve or something. Suddenly he's a little homesick for the old Willys and its canvas top and game four-banger engine.

The GTO is over on the shoulder of the road, and Perry parks next to it. The GTO is blue, and there's a large decal with Woody Woodpecker on it pasted to the rear window of the passenger side. Woody Woodpecker has his tongue stuck out and his eyes crossed in the picture.

There are about a dozen other cars there, and a state police cruiser and an ambulance. A group of men stand at the top of the bluff, holding cords that are tied to the searchers on the face. Perry thinks that one of them is the hefty trooper who watched them salvage the beef truck, but he isn't sure.

Weasel is there as well, but he isn't holding a rope. He's kneeling at the edge, calling down his advice. "Go left," he says. "Slide about a dozen feet to your left. This is a girl you're looking for. A girl is this big." He holds his hands about five feet apart.

"I see you got that thing on the road," Perry says to Weasel. He gestures behind them at the GTO. The valley beyond the bluff is a narrow one, thickly wooded. At its foot Perry sees the fire road where the Barracuda landed, and a small stream that winds along beside it. There are no guard-rails up on the knob, and the lack of skid marks makes him think that the Barracuda must have been going full tilt when it plunged over the edge. No touch on the brakes at all.

Weasel makes a gesture of dismissal to the men below, who are ignoring him, and stands. He dusts his knees off. "I got the nitrous in, but I haven't tested it yet. I know one guy that used nitrous in his car and the next thing he knew there was flame coming out of his heater vents. Burned his car all up."

"It puts a strain on a vehicle, I hear."

"I wondered if you would come up here. Papaduke was up not too long ago, but he didn't want to have nothing to do with the search," Weasel says. "He took one look at that cliff and I knew he didn't have the stuff."

"Did they find anything yet?"

"Nothing but pieces of car. They found a rearview mirror with a pair of shoes tied to it and a headrest off one of the seats and the radiator fan. But no girl." This last he calls down the bluff. "I got all that stuff in a box in the back of the car. I figure I'll take it to the yard with me when I go."

"What happened that they went over the edge?" Perry asks.

"Who knows? The guy was some kind of a daredevil, I guess. He never even touched his brake, is what they're saying. Went off the edge like it was some kind of a stunt."

Someone approaches them. It is the trooper from up on Big Lime, but he is in his civilian clothes, which is why Perry failed to recognize him. He isn't wearing a hat, and Perry sees that he is completely bald, figures he shaves his head. His thumbs are hooked in his wide leather belt. He grins when he sees Perry.

"Well, I'll be dogged. If it ain't the wrecker man," he says. He looks at Weasel. "And his friend Rabbit."

Weasel says, "Weasel."

The trooper says, "Whatever."

Perry holds his hand up. "We're just here to help," he says. "Not on business. We heard there was a search party on for a girl here. We just want to do what we can."

"Which is not much," the trooper says.

A shout goes up among the searchers. They have found the girl. Someone calls out that they need a saw to free her. As they suspected, she's caught in the branches of a tree.

"Is she alive?" one of the ambulance attendants calls down. He has a medical pack slung over his shoulder, like he is ready to rappel down there to her. He calls again, "Is she alive?" There is no answer to his question from the searchers, and the EMT shrugs, walks back to the ambulance, and lights a cigarette. Someone else ties a rope around himself and descends the bluff with a saw in his hands.

"There you are," the trooper says. "No need for your help at all."

Weasel acts as though he wants to leave, makes for the GTO, but Perry stands where he is, and Weasel drifts back to his side after a moment.

The girl comes slowly up the bluff, borne on the shoulders of four of the searchers. They strain against the ropes that hold them, and the men at the top of the cliff bring them in hand over hand. Several other men follow, some of them with more pieces of the car in their hands, one carrying the saw. The girl's limbs are loose. Her head hangs down and her dark hair trails on the ground. It is full of dirt and twigs and bits of tree.

One of the men who carries her is Lou, the young trooper. He is dressed in his civvies, like the older trooper. The expression on his face as he hauls himself upward is grim. He is not winded as the other men are but climbs among the rocks as if he were born to the exercise.

One of the girl's long pale legs is slung over his shoulder, and he avoids looking at her, keeps his eyes focused on the rock rim and the rope men above him. Her short denim skirt is rucked up on her thighs, and her blouse is open and torn. Her body continually threatens to slip away from the men and slide back down toward the bottom.

As the girl rises over the edge, the ambulance driver and his men take hold of her arms and shoulders, load her onto a wheeled stretcher. The climbers sit or stretch out on the ground, gasping for breath, some of them nearly weeping from exertion. Lou stands at the stretcher and smooths the girl's skirt down over her white cotton panties, closes her shirt as best he can.

"What a waste, eh, Lou?" the older trooper says. Lou makes no reply. Watching Lou fool with this dead girl's clothes has shaken Perry, and his spit tastes sour in his mouth. The features of her face are coarse, composed in an expression that's almost restful. He doesn't approach the stretcher, because he doesn't want to see where the tree branches have punctured her.

The ambulance men fold the girl's arms against her chest and trundle her off. One of the searchers, who must be a relative, rises with difficulty and climbs into the van beside her for the ride down to the county hospital. The ambulance has to back and fill to turn around on the narrow road, and the troopers move out into the road to stop oncoming traffic. Finally the ambulance switches on its flashers and pulls away.

"Let's get out of here," Weasel says. He goes to the GTO, climbs in, cranks the engine. The car's dual pipes roar and burble. The older trooper taps Lou on the shoulder and gestures at Weasel. Lou leans into the driver's window.

"Speed kills," he says.

"Yes sir," Weasel says.

"You keep this funny car reined in, son, or your ass belongs to me," Lou says.

Weasel is having some trouble framing a reply, and Lou stands away from the GTO and waves him on. Weasel reverses a short distance, backs into Perry's Impala. There is a sound like a tin can collapsing.

Weasel looks at Perry, his eyes wide. Perry nods at him not to worry, and Weasel accelerates, pulls away from them.

The chrome of the Impala's bumper is crimped a little on one side, but there's no significant damage.

"Looks like your friend got you," the older trooper says. "Want me to write him up?" Around them, the searchers are leaving, making plans to get a beer, have some supper.

"No," Perry says. "I don't want you to do anything." He begins to pick up the car parts that the searchers have scattered at the top of the cliff. Lou bends to help, but the older trooper stops him, and they get into their cruiser. In a minute they are gone.

Alone in that place, Perry is reluctant to leave. He wonders why the men on the cliff face brought these things up with them, wonders what parts they have left behind down there. There's a sideview mirror with the glass weirdly intact; the steering wheel, which is made of welded chain link; an inside door handle; a window crank.

The last thing that Perry retrieves is one of the Barracuda's hubcaps, which is made to resemble a wire wheel like an English racing car might have. He considers taking it with the other stuff, back to Mr. Papaduke, who would add it to his pile in the corner or tack it up on the wall with the others. He hefts it, then tosses it out over the bluff.

The hubcap flies beautifully when it leaves his hand, light as a tin pie plate. The wind catches it, and for a moment Perry imagines that it will spin out and out, across the valley and the fire road and the tame little stream, to land in the trees on the other side. Instead, abandoned by the breeze, it arcs suddenly downward and to his left, and disappears with a dull clang into the bushes somewhere below him, coming to rest in a tangled wooded place that he cannot see.

RESCUING
MOON

Mrs. Tencher checks me up and down. She is the lady that runs the place, and there is iron in her gaze. "Visiting hours is over," she says. "You just come back another time during the day and we'll see about letting you visit Mr. Potterfield." She don't like my looks any too much, that I can tell. I am a big man and never have been real what you would call presentable. Plus the ride over was hot and hard and I have sweated through my clothes under my arms and down my back, and that never does do much for the way you look.

"I come a long way, Mrs. Tencher," I say to her. She looks over my shoulder at where my old Dodge Dart is setting in the gravel drive. If it was a nice new Buick out there, or some kind of a foreign job, she'd let me in, but I know by the set of her mouth she don't like the primer paint or the places where the chrome is dead-looking and milky, like an eye that has got a cataract.

There is a couple scruffy-looking banty hens scratching near the car. As I watch, a little rooster with a tail like a feather duster comes out from behind a shed and jumps one of them. She squabbles like hell, but he just digs them sharp claws into her shoulder feathers and clips the back of her neck in his short beak and pushes her into the ground while he services her. The one hen screeches and tries to flap her pinned wings, loses a couple of feathers. The other hen has found a fat grub or something in the dust a couple feet away and don't seem to notice at all.

"Hell of a hard ride over them mountains, if you know what I mean," I say. I am still stiff from setting all that time. I work my shoulders. Mrs. Tencher, she don't like the sound of that "hell" too much, and her thick eyebrows knit together. She has been watching the birds out in the dirt of her yard, and she looks at me now with her sharp dark eyes. She is a big lady, wide across the shoulders and thick at the waist. She's got on a heavy canvas apron that's a mess down the front, looks like she's been butchering hogs in there.

"He wrote me, asked me to come," I say, and I hold the letter up, got my name on the front in Moon's hand—Grady Bell, Rural Route 4, Gilchrist—and him begging me to get him out of there. I hold it up in front of me like it is a writ or something. *You got to get me out of here, Grady*, the letter says. *What with the woman's food and her talk of God and keeping me all the time tied in the chair so I don't fall out she is like to put an end to me. I have not got long to go in this world without you should help*, it says.

That's enough for me. I don't leave home a whole hell of a lot, but that letter done it right there and got me going. So I stand where I am, facing down Mrs. Tencher herself on the steps of Mrs. Tencher's Manor for Adults. She don't look much like backing off, I am bound to admit.

An old man in a wheelchair rolls out on the porch where we are. His hair is white and his cheeks are sunk in. He's got him a false top plate that he keeps levering in and out of his mouth. Big yellow teeth, big square yellow fake teeth he's got. He nearly runs the chair into Mrs. Tencher when he comes up on her, wheeling it around pretty good with his skinny old arms. I see he is got one leg gone where his hospital johnny just folds up neat there.

"Mrs. Tencher," he says, real excited. He wheels the chair around her in a half-circle, and she turns to keep her eye on him, tries not to lose sight of me too. The hard rubber tires on the chair rumble over the loose boards of the porch. "Yo, Mrs. Tencher," he says, spinning the chair back toward her with one hand. I still got that letter held out in front of me and she hasn't even looked at it. I fold it in half, shove it back in my pocket.

"What is it, Colonel Combs?" she says to the man in the chair, and I can tell from her tone that Colonel Combs won't be getting raisins in his hot cereal for some time to come. He has pissed Mrs. Tencher off with bothering her, and no lie about that.

"Can't you see that I am talking with someone?" she says. She wedges a foot against the tire of old Combs's wheelchair to keep him in one place. "Colonel Combs is a veteran of the First World War," she says to me, like she needs to explain where his leg has gone, like I might think she took it off or something.

"He done it again, Mrs. Tencher," Combs says. "He got loose and stood up out the chair and now he's down and can't get back up. I figure might be he's busted his hip this time. All the noise he's making, awful noise." This seems like the most exciting thing that has happened to Combs in a while. I guess when you are as old as that and lost a leg to a war a long time ago, things get solemn for pretty lengthy stretches at a time.

Mrs. Tencher turns back to me and like to kill me with that look in her eye. I expect her to spit on me. "That'll be your Mr. Potterfield," she says. "He is all the time doing that kind of thing, and it'll be the end of him, him and me both," she says. She is already got that big body in motion across the porch. She skirts around Combs and into the house, and the screen door slams shut behind her. I hear her thumping on into the house and I am not sure just what I should do.

For a couple of minutes then it is just me and old Combs out there on the porch. I look at him and he looks at me. He is grinding that upper plate in his mouth. He hasn't moved the chair since Mrs. Tencher put the block on him.

The evening is a warm one. There are tree frogs all around the house, up there in the hills of Dwyer County, and they make a hell of a racket. It is a good summer sound, them tree frogs. The rooster has moved on to the other hen now, but she is quieter and gives in to him without a problem. The first hen has gone back to her yard-scratching.

"Well, Colonel Combs," I say, and I climb onto the porch where he is. "I expect I'll just go in and see about Mr. Potterfield."

Old Combs don't have any argument with that. He is just chewing that upper plate still. "He shouldn't ought to get out of the chair like that," he says to me. "I bet he busted his hip this time," he says. His eyes are bright blue in his weathered face. He looks at me like it is something real important he wants to say but just can't manage to get it out somehow.

"Might could be," I say. I push past him. The screen door is loose on its hinges and makes quite a noise as I go in. A spring slams it shut behind me. Looking outside, I can see

Combs has rolled his chair to the steps, craned his head so he can see out into the yard. Maybe it is the chickens that have got him so interested.

Toward the back of the house I can hear Mrs. Tencher's voice hectoring at somebody, and I figure that must be Moon. I hope he hasn't busted his hip and got to listen to Mrs. Tencher too. The house is dark, like they are saving electricity or maybe waiting for full night before they switch on.

I pass a room on the left and I can see it is a couple of Mrs. Tencher's adults in there too, looking out at me, one in a single bed against the wall, the other in a cane-back chair in the corner.

"Hey, O. John," the one in the bed says to me as I go by. I lean into the room. "I ain't O. John," I say to the man. He is holding one long arm out to me. "Sorry," I say. The one in the chair is a woman with a basket in her lap. She is knitting, moving the needles back and forth, back and forth in her crabbed old hands. I wonder how it is she can see to knit like that with the room as dark as it is.

"Hey, O. John," the old man says to me again.

"Never mind him," the old woman in the chair says, and her hands don't stop their shuttling, don't even let up for a minute. "He don't know what he's saying. Don't know who he's saying it to neither."

"Come on in here, O. John," the old man says. His voice is like sandpaper on hardwood, just a buzz and a rasp in his throat. It is like the ghost of a voice.

"Out of his head, huh," I say to the woman. I'm not even sure the old man is looking at me, seems like he's looking over my shoulder now, out into the empty hall, where it is all just shadows getting longer.

"He's got ears, though, don't he?" the woman says. She

stops knitting and stares hard at me, and I figure she is right. There is no call to talk about people that way. "Sorry," I say again and duck out of the room fast.

I can still hear Mrs. Tencher in the back of the house and I go toward where her voice is coming from. Having met some of the folks he is staying with, I am more ready than ever to get old Moon out of this place. This is no place for a man like Moon, that was a woodsman and a hunter as he was, with crazy old men that talk to people that ain't even there and Mrs. Tencher on you all the time.

I go in the room where Mrs. Tencher is, and Moon is in there too, setting in his own wheelchair and scowling at her. He has got the one light in the room on, a standing lamp with a tasseled cloth cover. There is a little triangular tear in the lampshade that throws a strong beam of light across his chest. He don't see me yet. I look him over, see where he is rubbing a hand on his leg, but nothing looks like it is busted. I am glad to see that.

It is the best thing about him, though. He has lost weight since he come up here, a lot of weight, and his skin has gone yellow. I don't like that at all. His mouth is pinched and looks mean, and she has got his hair cut back to nothing, like he is a recruit in the military. His ears stand out from his head like they do on the boys they got up on the farm at Huttonsville or in the maximum security at Moundsville.

"To control body vermin" is what he told me in one letter, and I known that was just the way she tried to sell it to him. I could see from the way the handwriting slanted across the page in big dark letters that it made him mad as hell to have to sit still for something like that.

"You horn-headed bitch," Moon says, and I never heard him talk to a woman like that before. "Why is it you are all the time messing with me?" His voice is soft, like he can't even draw the breath to shout at her. I think, this is the man that used to shout from one holler to another, used to call the hogs in a voice so strong and loud you'd think it was some kind of a church organ, all stops out.

"You got to stay in your chair, Mr. Potterfield," she says to him, sounding real reasonable. She has wrestled him back into his seat, no busted bones and no trouble. She don't see me behind her either, don't seem to be thinking of me at all.

"You got no use of them legs, so you got to sit. You can understand that. That's why we keep you tied in there, so you don't slip down." I can see where they got the johnny laced into the chair in back. It drives Moon crazy, I know, makes him work at it and worry it till he finally gets it loose.

I move into the room, and Mrs. Tencher rares back, she is so surprised to see me. "Hey Moon," I say. "I'm here to get you." I come right out with it, no use to beat around the issue. I figure maybe we can get this thing over with and get out of here soon, tonight. Looking at the way Mrs. Tencher has got her jaw set, though, I am not so sure it will be as easy as all that. She has still got that greasy canvas apron on, and it makes her look like she means serious business.

"Grady," he says. "Grady, goddamn, Grady." It is not much of a greeting, but I know what he means. He is glad to see me, but he never really expected to. It hurts me in a way that he did not expect me all along. He reaches up a hand and I take it. His flesh is cool and thin on the bones, hardly cushions them at all. Still, the bow-hunting calluses are there, rough and hard as a wood knot. I remember them calluses like they was on my own hands.

When I was a kid, Moon taught me all about the bow, how to stand quiet among the trees and pull back to full draw without quivering. He taught me the stance, the release, he showed me. Moon could put a shaft through the pumps of a whitetail at seventy yards, a perfect center-shot, and track the deer to wherever it might go down, across shale slides, through streams, up viney wooded grades. He come as close to being a Shawnee tracker as a white man is like to get. He was something to see, him and his shiny black bow, the one glove on his right hand with the palm cut out.

He was with me when I broke the back on my first decent buck, watched me put the four-bladed broadhead right into the spine at the withers. He clapped me on the back with that hand, full of strength and steady as you could want. I recall how that deer smelled when I knelt down next to it, the great warm body on that cold, cold day, and Moon standing beside me. I was just nothing but a young kid then. He pointed the fleas out to me where they were leaving the corpse, headed to who knows where, some other deer, maybe, that they could live on.

"Just like the frigging Marines," Moon says to me, licking his dry lips, not looking at Mrs. Tencher. "I known you wasn't just throwing them letters away. I known you was gonna come." It ain't the truth. He didn't know I was going to show up. The way he said that to Mrs. Tencher—"horn-headed bitch"—he was like a man that is fighting for his life, trying to hang on to something. Not much like a man that figures he is about to be rescued.

"You bet," I say.

Mrs. Tencher is right up behind me now. "I thought I told you, it ain't visiting hours," she says into the back of my neck.

"You getting me out of here?" Moon says. It looks to me like there are tears in the corners of his eyes, and I don't want to see the old man cry. He has been through enough up here that he shouldn't have to weep like some woman out in the open, in front of me and Mrs. Tencher and all. It makes me ashamed for him, like I had seen the man piss his pants or something.

It is strange to feel that about Moon Potterfield, that is a man I have looked up to all my life and learned a hell of a lot from, more than I ever learned in school. It is a lesson to me in what the years can bring a man to. He is fragile and sick, and suddenly it comes to me that maybe this is where he needs to be after all, maybe he needs the care that some home like this can give him. Too late for that kind of thinking, though. After I told him about getting out.

"Come to take you with me," I say.

"You ain't going to do any such thing," Mrs. Tencher says. She is standing her ground between me and the door, got her arms folded across her chest. "He ain't going to do any such thing," she says to Moon. Then she gets back to me. "What are you that you come in here and think you can do like this? This here's my place," she says.

I figure Moon is worth some dollars to her every month, some from his daughter in Memphis that found this place when his legs went bad and put him in it, some from the state. Mrs. Tencher must figure she is entitled to that money. She probably takes Moon's little railroad pension that he gets every month too, come to that.

"I tried calling you, Grady," Moon says. "I got on the horn and tried to get you, but it wasn't no use." He looks at Mrs. Tencher. "She kept all the time stopping me."

"The fee don't include long distance phone charges," Mrs. Tencher says. "If I just let somebody run up their bills on the phone all the time, then where'd I be? He didn't pay for no phone privileges," she says, pointing at Moon.

"It wouldn't of mattered, Moon," I say. "I got no phone up at the camp now anyway. They took it out."

Mrs. Tencher laughs like everything she has thought about me all along has just been proved. "A man that don't even have a phone," she says.

"He's my boy," Moon says to her in that quiet, wore-out voice. He don't mean that I am his son, because I am not, but just someone that grew up near him and learned from him. It is strange to hear that, thirty-four years old and still boy to this old man in the chair.

"Is he now," she says, and her eyes narrow. "I didn't know nothing about a boy. Your son, you say?"

Neither of us says anything back to her, and she don't get out of the doorway. I can see someone moving in the hall behind her. It is a girl moving out there in the dark house, coming from the kitchen. She steps past Mrs. Tencher into the room, and I see she has got on one of them thick aprons too, with gore down the front and on her chest. I think, What the Christ are they up to in there?

The girl is young, in her teens maybe, and a pretty soft blonde. Behind the apron—she has got it tied tight at the waist—I can see that her body is awful ripe, the kind of ripe that makes a man look twice, think twice. She holds something out toward me, a tiny little body with no hair, like something out of a dream. At first I think that it is a baby.

"We got rabbit, Mr. Potterfield," she says to Moon, and I see she is not looking at me at all. She holds the skinned rabbit out for Moon to see. "I know you like game meat, Mr. Potterfield. You always told me that you liked it. You wasn't lying to me, Mr. Potterfield."

"You get back in the kitchen, Ellen," Mrs. Tencher says to her. "This is between Mr. Potterfield and me," she says.

"A boy snared them and come around selling them. Your friend could stay to supper too if he wanted," Ellen says, but still she don't look at me. "We got plenty of them rabbits back in there."

I can picture her flaying a rabbit, with the sharp slender skinning knife tight in her hand. Even doing that she looks good to me, this soft little girl with the blood down her front. It gives me a tight feeling in my throat, how round her face is, how clean her hair looks tucked back behind her ears. I wonder what she is doing way back in these hills with all these old people in the dark. She should be somewhere else, that I know, but where it is exactly and how she might get there I couldn't say.

"She's a pretty, ain't she, Grady?" Moon says to me. He knows what I am thinking. Has always known, seems like. "I guess that's all I'll miss about this place, Grady, is Ellen and her sweet behind." It embarrasses me to hear Moon talk like that about a woman that is in the room with us, but she just smiles at him like it is an old joke between them.

"His friend won't be staying," Mrs. Tencher says to Ellen.

"You got that right," I say. I push against Moon's wheelchair, try to shove it toward the door, but it won't roll. The rubber tires screech against the wooden floor. Moon reaches a hand down, unlocks the wheels. I roll the chair toward Mrs. Tencher, and at first she don't move. I think I am going to have to go over her or through her or something to get out of here. Last minute, she backs out of the way. Ellen moves too.

"You ain't going nowhere," Mrs. Tencher says. She tugs at the back of my shirt, but we are past her now, headed toward the front of the house. As we pass that first room, I can hear the constant *click, click, click* of the old lady's knitting needles. "O. John," the old man says, but I know he is not talking to anybody that is nearby.

"That's O. John and his mother in there," Moon says. "He's all right."

"His mother," I say. "Shoot, I thought they was both around a hundred years old."

"You never can tell," Moon says. "She don't even need to be in here. She's just here to look after O. John."

Then I bang Moon's chair through the front door and we come out into the evening air, out where we can hear the tree frogs singing. "Good boy," Moon says to me. Looking down, I can see his scalp through the brush-cut hair, as yellow and unhealthy as the rest of him. "How do you like that, Tencher, you old whore," he says back over his shoulder, and it is the loudest thing I heard him say yet.

"You are killing that old man, sure as the day," Mrs. Tencher says behind me. Old Combs, sitting out on the porch all this time, wheels his chair around to face me and Moon. He looks at us and his face is long. "Going somewheres?" he asks.

"Getting out," Moon says. "Getting the hell out."

"Shoot," Combs says. "I wish you luck," he says. I stop the chair so that he can talk, and Mrs. Tencher slows up behind us, breathing hard. Combs looks at the floorboards. "You ain't going to get much of anywhere, I would say, but I sure do wish you luck."

"You always was a cheerful son of a bitch," Moon says. He bangs on the arms of the chair. "Get this chariot rolling, Grady," he says.

It takes me a minute to manhandle Moon's chair down the uneven porch steps. Having Mrs. Tencher right behind me like that makes me nervous. One of the steps gives a little and I am scared that I will pitch down on top of him, knock him out of the chair. Up on the porch Combs is looking after us, fondling the stump of his leg.

Mrs. Tencher is still coming after us, past Combs, down the stairs. "Get Colonel Combs inside," she says to Ellen, who comes after her. Ellen just stands on the top step, watching. She has still got the rabbit in her hand, holding it by the hind legs.

"You going to give him his pills?" Mrs. Tencher says to me. "Who's going to give that man his pills? Not you, that's who," she says. "Eight different kinds of pills he's got to have, the doctor says, four different times of day. You going to do that for him?"

I don't say anything back, just keep the chair rolling toward the car. I don't want to get in a wrestling match with her. "Coot," Moon says back to her. "Bunch of coots," he says again, softer.

"Hush," I say. "Let me get us out of here."

"Help me get in the car," Moon says. "I got no use of my legs. You got to lift me in."

"What about them pills, Moon?" I say. It strikes me as something to think about.

"I don't need no pills," he says. "Get me in the car."

"No pills," Mrs. Tencher says. "Stone dead inside of a fortnight, a week, is what. Dead and mortifying. You watch."

I untie the hospital johnny, lift Moon up out of the chair. He is light as a girl, and his head is heavy on his neck, I can see. There is no strength or weight to him. His flesh is dry and cool, like the skin of a snake. It is not easy to open the car door, but I get it done, put Moon in the passenger seat. He slumps down, and I belt him in as tight as I can to keep him sitting up. "Hell of a job," he says to me. "Keep it up." I shut the car door.

"It'll be on your head," she says. "When he grabs his chest

and coughs up blood, that'll weigh on you. You'll carry that crime before Almighty God," she says.

I pay her no attention, even though she is shouting it in my ear. For a minute I am confused what to do with the wheelchair. I see that it folds up and wonder about putting it in the trunk.

"Don't you even think about that," Mrs. Tencher says. "You take the old man if you want him, but that wheelchair belongs to me. Didn't nobody pay me for that wheelchair."

I leave the chair where it sets.

"Don't you worry, Mrs. Tencher," I say to her. With Moon out of the picture and not cussing her for a minute, I figure to calm her down somewhat. "He'll be all right."

"I ain't worried," she says, and her face is contorted and ugly, she is so angry. The cords on her neck stand out. "You're the one that's got to be worried. You're the one that's killing him."

I get in the driver's side, crank the car up. Mrs. Tencher stands next to her wheelchair, staring at me and Moon in the car. I can smell him in the seat next to me. No matter how a man tries, he can never keep real clean in a place like that, with not being able to take a real bath and all. He smells like sick-sweat and alcohol rub. Smells like a vet's waiting room.

As I back the car around, I see Ellen still up on the porch, next to Colonel Combs. He is rocking his chair back and forth like with nerves, tapping that one foot. Ellen is as angry as Mrs. Tencher now that she sees she isn't going to be able to keep us, now that she knows we are going to get away with it. I am surprised to see that, such a pretty girl and so mad. She shakes her head, scowling. We will not eat her game meat that she has taken such pains over.

She underhands the skinned rabbit at the car, and it

smacks the windshield right in front of my face, sounds like a softball. It bounces off, lays in the gravel next to the car, pale against the rocks. A couple busted bones poke out of the flesh. There is juice on the windshield where it hit.

"Jesus Christ," I say, shoving the Dodge into drive. "That's a crazy thing to do."

The left rear tire goes over something small, something that makes a crunch. Mrs. Tencher cries out. For a second I am sure it is her foot that I have run over. She slams a fist down on the rear quarter-panel of the car.

Looking in the rearview, I see her bent over the feathers, the bright tailfeathers of the banty rooster. I put the wheel right over him without even meaning to. I can see where a small breeze shivers the feathers as Mrs. Tencher cries over them. I am surprised to see the tears on her face. I put on the brakes, start to get out of the car.

"You crazy?" Moon says to me. "You don't want to go back there. She'll kill you. She loved that goddamn chicken."

"Yeah," I say. He is right about that. As we pull out of the yard, onto the nine-foot blacktop, I see that Mrs. Tencher has straightened up, is shaking that fist after us, shouting. I can't hear what it is she says.

"Shoot," Moon says. He is laughing. He has seen it all, and sick as he is, he is laughing to bust a gut.

"What is it!" I say. "Christ, I don't see what's so funny." I turn on the windshield wipers to try and get the rabbit blood off the windshield, but it just smears and makes it worse.

"Goddamn," he says. He is wiping at his eyes and it is good to see him this happy, even if I am not sure what is funny. Looking behind us, I can see Ellen wheeling Combs back into the Manor. Mrs. Tencher is down on the ground, got her hand in the little pile of feathers, not even looking after us anymore. I set the car straight on the road and grind all the speed out of it that I can get.

"I don't know about you killing this old man," Moon says, and he is still laughing, "but you sure as hell did leave that woman's yard full of little dead animals, didn't you?"

He settles his head back against the seat like he is going to sleep. Looking at him, with his sunken eyes and skin parched like a mummy, I get the image of what he will look like when he is dead. The road stretches out ahead of me, all the way across the mountains and the big level to the camp on the Jackson.

What then, I want to ask Moon, but he is shaking a little like he is laughing inside. What about when we get back to the camp, I want to say, but there is no good answer he could give me. That is a question that I will have to answer somehow myself, some other time. And I think, Right now it is some driving I have got to do.

WASHMAN

Gandy Dolan was sitting out on the porch with his girl when Washman went by. Washman was riding a mule, and the mule was old and grizzled and it moved its legs in clumsy cadence, like it was remembering how to walk with every step. It was a jug-headed mule, and its ears were ragged where other pack animals had savaged it. Gandy Dolan pushed the girl off his lap and walked to the edge of the porch. He put his hands on his lean hips, said, "Jesus Christ that's ugly."

Washman didn't raise his head off his chest at the insult, and he didn't cluck at the mule to speed its pace. To Gandy Dolan it looked like Washman had his eyes shut. It looked like Washman was asleep there astride the mule. Gandy stepped down off the porch and trotted along at the mule's shoulder. The road was an inch deep with a foul muck and Gandy's feet sank into it and slipped in the wheel ruts and the going was harder than he had thought it would be. The girl watched from the porch as Gandy and Washman and the mule proceeded down the road away from her.

"That thing ought to be shot," Gandy said to Washman. "A mercy to it and a mercy to us not to have to look at it," he said.

Washman still didn't raise his head from his chest. He was a hunchback with a large head and a thick squat body and long mighty arms and little legs that didn't go very far around the barrel of the mule's ribs. In his gear he carried a pair of thick varnished sticks that he used to help him walk.

Washman's legs swung bonelessly with the mule's rocking gait. It occurred to Gandy that maybe Washman was dead and still perched on his mule, and that the mule was bearing the corpse away to some solemn haunted place. The idea chilled Gandy, and he stopped following.

Then he looked up at the porch of his house and saw that the girl was watching him. There was no readable expression on her face. She wasn't amused and she wasn't scared, and Gandy thought that she didn't much care what he did. He turned and splashed down the road and caught up with Washman's mule again. It had gone about a quarter of a mile past the house.

Gandy grabbed at the rope halter that hung on the mule's mostly hairless head and dragged down on it. The mule took a couple steps more, dragging Gandy along, and for a second he thought that it wasn't going to stop for him. Then it balked and shook its head and bared its teeth. He snatched his hand away. The mule laid its long ears back and brayed.

Washman's head came up and he opened his eyes. He had great deep-set slate-colored eyes with thick lashes. A woman a long time ago had told him that she could almost love him for his eyes, that they were gentle and could just about make her forget the strangeness of his crippled, corded body.

"What the hell," Washman said.

Gandy moved around in front of the mule and stood in its way. He crossed his arms over his chest. He was a young man, and good-looking, and gorgeously dressed. He wore a silk shirt and tight cotton trousers tucked into tall, glossy boots. The boots were stained with filth from the road. He had on a short vest embroidered with bright metal thread and a black bowler hat that was a little too small for his head. A crest was sewn onto the pocket of Gandy's shirt, a golden bird in a wash of flame, but it had nothing to do with Gandy.

Gandy was a highwayman and he had stolen the shirt, and he had stolen all the other fine clothes he was wearing. He got them out of a heavy silver-bound trunk that he had hoped was full of payroll money. It had been a moonless night and cold and raining and illuminated only by occasional strokes of lightning. Gandy had shot a man over that trunk. He couldn't believe that anybody had fought so hard over a box of clothes. He found out later that the man was some kind of a Spanish don from Sonora, so he wore the don's togs.

"Listen," Gandy said to Washman. "You go by my house. You go by my house on this road from time to time, coming from wherever it is you come from, and you always go at the same pace, and you never vary that pace as I watch you." Gandy shifted from foot to foot, and his head was down as he talked. "On the day that you go past, from the morning until the night, all I can do is sit around my house and wait on you. I know you'll be coming back on this same road at the same pace that night."

Washman kicked at the mule to start it forward again,

and he made a clicking sound with his tongue. Gandy stood his ground, with his right hand in front of him, palm out.

"Hold it," he said. "I wait around my house, and I can't get to sleep until you go by. And then when you do come I watch you riding your hideous mule that staggers when it walks, and if there's a moon I just let it light you up, and if there's no moon I get a bull's-eye lamp and I shine that light on you. Dark night or moonlight, you go past here and I watch you and sometimes even after you've gone I can't sleep for thinking about the sight." He lowered his outstretched hand.

"I notice that light you put on me," Washman said. He had a baritone voice that sounded like it came from far inside his massive chest. "I wondered what it was you wanted."

"Listen," Gandy said again, then he was quiet. He stood there looking at the mud that caked his magnificent boots. After a minute Washman decided he wasn't going to say anything, and he figured there must be some sound he was supposed to listen to. He cocked his head but heard nothing special. There was a light spring wind in the oaks around Gandy's place, and the morning whir of grasshoppers, and a dog barking at intervals off in the deep heart of the woods, but nothing else.

"You do what you want," Gandy said at last, and now he was looking straight at Washman, "but me, I've got to shoot your awful mule." He drew a heavy silver-plated revolver from under the short vest. It was a modified Navy dragoon, with grips made of elephant ivory. Gandy had taken it off the Spanish don's body.

The grips were carved with the bas-relief figures of rampant elephants, one on the left and one on the right. The twin elephants were lifelike—so detailed that you could make out their tiny piggy eyes and their hairless tails and even the wrinkled baggy skin of their knees—and they delighted Gandy. Sometimes he would clench the revolver tight for a while and then open his hand and marvel at the elephant imprinted on his palm. He thumbed back the hammer of the dragoon and put the muzzle next to the mule's head. The mule twitched an ear but held fast.

"Why don't you just stop looking?" Washman said. "Why don't you go inside?"

"I tried that," Gandy said. "I hear you coming in the morning, so I go in the house where I won't have to see. Then when I'm inside and I'm looking at something else—a photograph or my girl's bare breasts or the flame of a candle—I begin to wonder if it really is you again." He took a deep breath, went on. "Of course I know it's you from your mule's terrible tread, but I start to doubt what I know and finally I have to come out and see it. And there I am." Gandy's hand trembled, holding the cocked revolver at the mule's earhole.

"I seen the girl," Washman said. His hand wandered back behind him to the stock of the gun he kept there. It was a double-barreled .52 caliber gun with smooth bores. He carried it in a leather scabbard across the mule's hips. The scabbard was lashed to the leather panniers the mule carried, close to Washman's busted saddle.

"She watches me as I go by too," he said to Gandy. "She stands in a window on the second floor of the house, and oftentimes she's naked when she stands there." He looked at Gandy, who was holding the dragoon with both his hands to steady it. "Where did you get her?" Washman asked.

"I stole her," Gandy said. He paused. "I won her in a card game in Nacogdoches, but I was cheating, so it's the same as if I stole her."

Washman freed his gun from its scabbard as Gandy spoke, brought it around his body, and leveled it at Gandy's chest. He pulled back the twin hammers with the flat of his left hand. Gandy went on talking.

"The guy I won her from came after her, though. We were living in a house in Tennessee at the time and I had a different name. How he found us I don't know. He couldn't live without her. He sang under the window at night, only he didn't know which window was hers, so he sang under every window in the place. He sang Italian love songs to her."

"I would take another road into town if there was one," Washman said. He rested the double-barreled gun on the mule's wither, and the skin there quivered at the touch of the cool metal. "But there's no other way around, and I need this mule."

"We would screw while he was singing," Gandy said, "and we laughed at him from under the covers. She thought it was funny that he lost her in a rigged game. She thought it was funny that he sang to her."

"I'll trouble you to put down your piece," Washman said. Gandy took no notice of him.

"One night he climbed up the side of the house somehow and got a window open and started to crawl in. He was singing all the way up, and by the time he got to the top he was out of breath and the song was barely a whisper."

"Shut up and step away," Washman said.

"I had a piece of thick oak board. I waited on him just to one side of the window. He came in and I battered him and finally he just gave up his grip. He slipped outside and went down the wall of the house and he lay out there crying. About midnight the moon came up and he screamed real loud."

Gandy imitated the scream. He made it sound like the cry of the dog in the woods, a high-pitched yelp, and the mule flinched and laid its ears along its skull again. Washman tightened his finger on the front trigger of his gun.

"When I looked out in the yard the next day, he was gone," Gandy said. "That guy never did come back."

The two men stayed where they were for a moment and regarded each other. Gandy seemed to take in Washman's gun for the first time. He examined the brutal dark length of it. "A fellow tried to sell me one of those in a bar in Oklahoma," he said. "He was a little old bony fellow and he said he was a buffalo hunter back before the herds dried up."

"I imagine this evens the odds somewhat," Washman said.

"No, I don't think so," Gandy said. "I bet that thing don't even shoot anymore." He grinned and swung the dragoon to bear on Washman.

"Wrong," Washman said, and he squeezed the front trigger. The left hammer of the gun fell and the percussion cap popped and that was all. A trace of smoke rose from under the hammer.

Gandy stood there and he laughed at Washman. He threw back his head and laughed and he lowered the revolver to his side. Washman pulled the second trigger and the right hammer fell, and this time the gun went off. The slug hit Gandy in the chest just below the crest on his shirt and to the right of it.

The force of the round shoved Gandy backward, and his feet dragged in the mud. He fought to stay upright. He closed his eyes, opened them, and he saw that Washman and the mule were farther away than he thought they should be. They seemed to be ringed with light. As Gandy watched, Washman ran another load into the right barrel of his gun, recapped the left, and Gandy understood that Washman planned to shoot him again.

His shirt was burned in a dozen different places, and so was his vest, and he was polluted from the waist up with spent gunpowder. He saw the hole in the shirt, and he knew that it was a hole in his chest as well. Smoke curled out of the hole, and it looked to him just like the smoke from Washman's misfire.

Gandy raised the don's silver-plated dragoon and snapped off a shot, took a chunk out of one of the mule's ears. The mule sat down, and Washman rolled off. Gandy fired again, and the round spun off into the sky. He fired the revolver a third time, and the bullet struck Washman low in the ribs. Then Gandy fell and lost the revolver in the mud of the road, and he had no strength to go searching after it.

Washman fought his way to his feet, leaning against the seated mule. He had kept his grip on the gun. He trained it on Gandy, who was face down in the road. Gandy was making a terrible moaning sound, and Washman thought that probably his mouth was filled with mud.

Gandy's hand was stretched toward the revolver, but Washman was satisfied that he couldn't reach it and that he wouldn't rise again. Gandy moved his arms and his legs in a helpless swimming motion. Then the legs stopped, and only his arms moved. In a minute they ceased too, and he lay still. Washman mounted the mule painfully and slapped it with his open hand until it stood. He turned it and headed back up the road to Gandy's house.

The girl was waiting for him when he got there. She was young, dressed in a long white nightdress decorated with silver ribbons. It had belonged to the mistress of the Spanish don, and Gandy had given it to the girl. Her feet were bare, and the dress hung loose on her slim body. She had green slanted eyes and sallow skin and short dark hair that was cut like a man's.

She nodded down the road to where Gandy lay sprawled. "Is he dead?" she said.

"Yes," Washman said to her. Just then Gandy cried out. He had turned his head to one side to get his mouth clear of the mud. Washman didn't take his eyes off the girl, but he colored, embarrassed to have been caught in a lie.

"He might as well be," he said. "He's got a hole in him you could pitch a cat through." Washman himself was in a good deal of pain and bleeding freely, but he was pretty sure that Gandy's bullet had passed straight on through him without getting anything important. He knew he could pack the wound later and he would be okay. Things like it had happened to him before.

"Climb up," Washman said to the girl, and he gestured at the mule's withers in front of him. "You'll come with me, I guess." Gandy was still making his noise, and Washman didn't care to have to listen to it anymore.

"I'm not sure that I will," the girl said. "What makes you think I'll do what you say?"

"Well," Washman said. He turned sideways in the saddle, pointed behind him. "I shot that one there. He was the one that had you and I've killed him. Or nearly."

The girl pursed her mouth. "So you killed him," she said. "That how it works with you?"

"That's how it works with you," Washman said. "He beat your Frenchman, and now I've beaten him."

"Italian."

"What?"

"He was Italian, an important family that fell on hard

times. They disowned him when he wanted to marry a pauper girl that he loved. They had some hag of a rich woman lined up for him, so he came to America," the girl said. "He was from Roma." She rolled the R prettily.

"We got to go," Washman said. "Get up here."

"He thought he was pretty slick. He thought he could play cards, but you could see everything in his face. It was like the cards were printed there, especially when he was drinking. He could never figure why he was getting beat. I could play better cards than he could."

Washman nudged the mule forward, and it put one front hoof up on the boards of the porch, then the other. Its heavy feet boomed against the wood.

"I don't believe I want to go with you anyhow," the girl said. "Where are you going to?"

"Upland," Washman said. He ducked his head to get beneath the eaves of the roof and sat astride the mule, half on and half off the porch. "Don't make me come after you."

"You couldn't come after me. It don't appear to me that you got much in the way of legs to chase a person with."

"The mule is my legs," Washman said. "It can go where you go, and a lot of places that you couldn't get to besides. You don't want me after you."

"You'd beat me if I was to make a run for it," the girl said.

"You'd regret it bitterly," Washman said.

The girl shrugged and sighed. "I'll want some things to take along," she said.

"All right," Washman said.

The girl started toward the door of the house, and then she came back to the mule. "I'll tell you one thing," she said, and she looked Washman up and down. The filth of the road clung to him, to his pants and his shirt and his cheeks and forehead, and to the gun that he clutched in one hand.

"I didn't know what exactly would kill the man," she said, "but I sure as hell didn't picture nothing like what did it." She turned and went inside.

Washman figured her agreement to be a ruse. He listened for her footsteps pounding out the back door and into the woods. He didn't know whether he'd be able to catch her or not if she bolted. He wasn't sure whether he planned to try.

While he waited, he cleaned the gun off as best he could and slid it back into its sheath. He clucked to the mule, backed it off the porch, bumping his head on the edge of the roof as he did.

The girl came back in a couple of minutes, carrying a rolled towel under her arm. She had the few things she wanted from the house wrapped in the towel. She wore a pair of black satin slippers on her feet. Washman turned the mule so she could mount it from the porch. She paused before she climbed on.

"You sure it can carry us both?" she asked.

Washman leaned over and caught her in his arms and lifted her and set her on the mule before him. She hiked up the nightdress and gripped the mule with her strong legs. It sighed and shifted its weight, bobbed its head. The girl looked at Gandy one final time. "He sure was pretty," she said.

"He was a fop," Washman said. He whistled to the mule, tugged the reins to guide it, and the three of them started the long trip back up the road, toward Washman's homestead in the highlands.

. . .

A man in a motorcar came up the road from Fort Terrance, which was the town toward which Washman had been riding. He was demonstrating the new car to his fiancée. It was a small vehicle with tall narrow rubber tires and wooden spokes in its wheels and brass carriage lamps clamped to the windscreen, and it smoked as it chugged and popped down the road.

The man wore a woven cap and an aviator's goggles and a pair of heavy leather gauntlets to drive in, and his fiancée wore a great flowered hat. Even though the hat tied under her chin, it blew off her head as they roared down the road away from town, and the woman was glad to feel it go. A car was a rare sight in that place in those times, and she felt honored to be riding in the high-backed, upholstered passenger seat. She didn't at all mind the mud that spun up from the wheels and spattered her clothes, or the rushing wind that ruined the careful design of her hair. Her heart was beating fast. The man slowed down as if to go back and get the hat, but the woman waved him on.

They almost ran right over Gandy Dolan. When the man saw the body in his path, he laid on the hand brake of the car, which slid across the road in the mud, tipping up on two wheels. For a second the man thought the car would go over on its side, and the woman shrieked as she was tossed from her seat. She landed on her knees and elbows, and her left arm went numb as she struck the ground. She rolled over a couple of times, fetching up against Gandy's body. She stopped screaming and lay with her forehead cushioned against his legs.

The man jumped out of the car and raced around it. When

he got to Gandy and the woman, he stood still, unsure as to what he should do first. He knelt next to the woman, lifted her head, pushed Gandy's legs out of his way. Gandy shouted when he was moved, but the man went on pushing. When he had got Gandy far enough away, he sat in the mud and took his fiancée's head in his lap. He moistened his handkerchief with his tongue and used it to wipe the worst of the soil from her face.

With her eyes still closed she spoke to him. "Who is he?" she asked.

The man continued to clean her face. "Your arm," he said. "Your splendid, splendid arm." He was afraid to touch her arm, which was swollen and bleeding. His father was a doctor in Fort Terrance, and the man prayed that she could be healed. He prayed that her arm wouldn't have to be amputated. She had lovely hands and darling round arms.

"To hell with my arm," she said, and she shoved herself to a sitting position. "My arm is fine," she said, though it felt like a stick of stovewood from her fingertips to an inch above her elbow. She looked at Gandy where he lay, on his side now. He was facing them, and his lips moved. He moaned and whispered and made strange barking sounds. There was a thin foam of blood on his lips. His shirt was soaked with blood that had leaked from the hole in his chest.

"My God," the woman said. "He's beautiful." The man thought that he had misheard her. He looked at the wretch lying in the road, and then he leaned in close to the woman.

"What?" he said.

"Put him in the car," she said. "We've got to take him into town."

"Put him in the car," the man said. Gandy had lapsed

back into unconsciousness. The man noticed the silver dragoon lying in the mud a few feet away from him. "He's got a gun," he said. "He's been shot, I'd say. There must have been a gunfight or something."

The woman sat up, gained her feet. Her knees stung, but she was able to stand, leaning on the car. The man picked up the revolver and hefted it. It was a good-looking weapon, an expensive one. He tucked it into his belt. Then he bent and scooped Gandy up. Gandy was big, but the man was strong and had no trouble carrying him to the car. The woman climbed into the narrow back seat. She told the man to put Gandy back there with her, and he did.

She cradled Gandy's head in her lap, brushed the matted hair off his forehead. His skin was pale and cool from blood loss and shock, and his lips were nearly blue. The woman bent over him and wondered at how fine his features were, at how thin the skin was that covered the excellent bones of his face. She ran her thumb down the bridge of his nose, and he smiled briefly at the sensation. She saw that his teeth were straight and clean and healthy. She felt that he was dying, and she had him all to herself for a brief time there in the back of the roadster.

The man kept looking over his shoulder at Gandy and the woman. Her head was close to Gandy's, and her long hair obscured his face and her own. Strands of the woman's hair streamed in the wind. She held her shattered arm stiffly out from her body. The man smiled grimly to himself, tugged his cap down lower on his forehead, and swore he would not look again until they were in the valley, in Fort Terrance.

The car rocked on its steel springs as it passed over the troughs and mounds in the road, and both the woman and Gandy across her knees cried out with every impact. When they came to the flowered hat the woman had lost, the man did not slow or stop. The offside wheels passed over the crown of the hat, tossing it out behind the car and into the weeds at the side of the highway, but the woman didn't look up from Gandy or notice the hat's destruction at all.

During his first night at the clinic in Fort Terrance, Gandy Dolan began to scream. Sometimes the screams were just the noise of his agony and rage. Sometimes they were names. He called out the name of his mother, which was Josephine, and the name that he had called the girl, which was Clementine, and the name he imagined for the woman who had kissed him in the back of the car, which was Lucille. The doctor, who was the father of the man with the car, tried to calm him, because every time he screamed he bled from his mouth and reopened the wound in his chest.

Washman's bullet had smashed through his sternum, damaged his lungs and his heart. It was lodged in his spine, impossible to remove. Gandy Dolan was paralyzed and bleeding heavily inside, and the doctor told anyone who asked that he was bound to die before another night fell. They asked because Fort Terrance was a small town clustered in a single hollow where Gandy Dolan's screams echoed and reverberated and never seemed to die away before he began to scream and sob again. While Gandy Dolan screamed out the names that he knew, it was impossible for any but the hardest of heart in the town to get a night's sleep.

Gandy didn't die the next night, or the night after that. He lived on and continued to scream, and his voice didn't grow hoarse or weak and his heart didn't simply burst from the effort, though people swore it had to give out soon, and any number of them wished that it would. He screamed like a baby that had colic, without cease or hope of comfort.

At some point he stopped calling out names, and he began to recite the events that had brought him to the cot in the corner of the clinic. The place was deserted because there was no one who could bear to stay in there with him, and the doctor's hands shook with nerves.

The woman from the car visited him twice a day, and she sat on a stool beside his bed and watched his body twist and arch beneath the soaked sheets, watched the contortions of his face and the blank staring of his eyes. She listened to him as he shouted out his names, and later as he raved about the hunchback and the ugly mule and the pale little girl with the man's haircut. The woman didn't know that he believed her name was Lucille, so she never corrected him or even knew that he had noticed her at all.

Her arm was splinted and wrapped from shoulder to knuckles and cruelly braced with metal. It pained her constantly, and Gandy's voice when she drew near him sent particular thrills of agony through the riven bone. She watched her fingers, the little of them that extended out of the bundle, turning black, and she knew that she would not use her arm again.

The woman brought Gandy food, but he would not eat or even recognize the offering, and he wasted there in his bed. The flesh fell off his bones until she could see clearly the faultless shape of the skull she had admired in the car. Finally she couldn't bear to be so close to his screaming. She went back to her own home, six houses down the street from the clinic.

She sat inside with the curtains drawn, and she tried to listen to nothing. She tried to imagine the world as it would have been if she had never seen Gandy Dolan or driven in a car. She tapped her awkward, fragile arm against the edge of her sewing table and tried to pretend that she was whole again.

The men came into the room where Gandy lay screaming: ten, eleven, twelve of them. They filled the place, and they sat around on the stools that were there, and on the edges of the cots, and they stared at the rigid form of Gandy Dolan. A couple of them clapped their hands to their ears to diminish the sound of his voice, but most of them were dulled to it and listened to his recitation in the sickroom with pained familiarity.

"It didn't go off," Gandy screamed. "I thought I had him. Had him cold. There on his damned mule. Wasn't paying attention."

The men weren't wearing hoods, and they carried no pistols or daggers or weapons of any sort. Still, the doctor backed away from them as though they were brigands or murderers and not people he knew in the daylight and did business with. He had treated their children for illness, and the men themselves, and he had watched their families grow and attended at those births. He had seen plenty of those children die as well, and any number of others, but he had no power in this group.

"You don't want to do this," the doctor said. "He's done nothing."

"Get out of here," one of the men said. It was the doctor's son who spoke. He wore a smile on his face like a terrible disguise.

"He's a man," the doctor said.

"Saw him coming," Gandy called. "Saw him coming. Saw him coming. Saw him coming."

"He's not a man," the doctor's son said. "He's just a noise.

The man died up there on the road, and his noise hasn't followed him yet."

"It's a murder," the doctor said.

"People are saying he'll never die," the doctor's son said. "They're saying that he'll just lie in here for the rest of time and scream."

"He'll die on his own," the doctor said.

"Not soon enough," his son said, and he started forward, and so did the other men. The doctor moved between them and the cot where Gandy lay. He spread his arms out.

"I won't let you do it," the doctor said.

"You don't have a choice in the matter," his son said, and he laid hands on the old man and shoved him to one side.

The other men grabbed the doctor, and they passed him from one to the other, and they swatted him, batted his glasses off his face, nicked his shins with their boots. Two of them pushed him through the door of the clinic. They were large men, and they knocked him to the ground and pinned him there. They were breathing hard as they kneeled on him and twisted his arms behind his back. He cried out. The clinic door closed.

The doctor heard Gandy say, "Ugly, ugly ears." Then the constant voice was muffled. Then it ceased.

Though he tried, the doctor couldn't make out the sounds of any struggle inside. A few minutes later the door to the clinic opened, and the doctor's captors freed him. He stood, brushed at his clothes with his hands, smoothed the sleeves of his coat. The men who had held him were his neighbors, and he couldn't look at them. The others emerged from the clinic, one by one, and as they came they looked around them, and they seemed to relish the unaccustomed silence that had fallen over Fort Terrance. They gathered together and con-

ferred for a minute, and then they set out for the mountains
to find the hunchback who had murdered Gandy Dolan.

The girl Gandy had called Clementine stood before Washman.
She had a big gold pocket watch in her hand, and she dangled
it by its chain. It was one of the things that she had brought
with her from the house in the valley. She flicked the watch
with her finger, and it spun. The sun danced on its bright
casing.

"It don't work," she said. "There's something wrong with
it."

Washman's back was turned to her. He leaned against the
mule's flank, holding its right forefoot between his warped
knees, filing the hoof. His canes were on the ground beside
him. Washman and the girl were in the shed that stood behind
Washman's two-room house. He had told the girl that he
raised up the whole homestead himself. She had asked him
why this place, and he showed her where a clear stream gushed
from a rock face two dozen paces from his door. That was
all the answer he gave her.

The mule's ear, the one that Gandy had put a bullet
through, was infected, and the side of the mule's head was
swollen. The girl thought it looked peculiar and comical with
the flesh all taut and bulbous on that side, and the one eye
squeezed shut. Washman had told her it would either cure
itself or it wouldn't.

Washman wore a plain cotton shirt and a jacket in the
cool highland morning. The jacket was tight across his broad
humped back. From behind him the girl couldn't see his head,
it hung so low. He grunted, put the mule's foot back on the
ground, picked up his canes. He turned to face her.

"What don't work?" he said.

"The watch," she said. "It runs backward sometimes, and then it runs forward but real, real slow. And one time yesterday I looked and it was running ahead of itself. The minute hand went around three times while I counted ten."

Washman took the watch from her and inspected it. There was a firebird design on the hinged cover, and Washman admired the filigree, but he didn't recognize it as a match to the crest on Gandy's silk shirt. He popped the heavy watch open, and a little music box inside played a waltz that he enjoyed. He imagined dancing to the tune with the girl, and wished that he had legs for dancing. He closed the watch and opened it again, and this time it played a different song. He smiled.

"It's got five songs that it plays," the girl said. "That part's working okay. It plays the tunes one right after the other."

Washman handed the watch back to her. "The clock part won't ever work here," he said. "I give up trying to have a clock in this place a long time ago. Use it for a music box, but don't bother keeping time with it. It's something in the rocks around here that jiggers the guts of a timepiece. It's a sort of magnetism."

"Magnetism," she said.

"The dirt's thin up here, and the rocks glow at night where they thrust up through it," he said. "The will-o'-the-wisp flits from rock to rock and is never still." He pointed to the watch. "And it's got in your little ticker there and played hell with it."

The girl spun away from him, whistling one of the watch's tunes. She had learned them all by heart sitting in the parlor of Gandy's house. They kept her company up here on the silent mountain and reminded her of those times. The strange spinning of the watch's hands had unhinged her notion of chronology, and she was not sure how long she had been with Washman.

The first night, after they had arrived at the little house, Washman had hauled her inside and stripped her and screwed her. He hurt her, and she screamed and fought him. She tried to tear at the bullet wound in his side, but he kept her away from it with his great hands like wooden paddles, and he struck her until she was dizzy and weak and sick from the blows.

The next night he had slept in the front room, in a heap on the floor. She thought he was sorry about the night before, but still she didn't sleep, listening to him turning over and over there in the next room, listening also to the coyotes that prowled outside and yelped and battled each other.

On the third night he came back again, and this time she bit his hand and ground the small bones between her teeth as he went to rut on her. The hand became infected, like the mule's ear, the wound tender and gray and weeping, and the injury had kept him away from her for a while. He had moved slowly in those days, and his skin was flushed and his eyes were hollow and reddened, and they seemed to stare at her from a long way off.

The hand had pretty well healed by the day she showed him the strange action of the watch, and he came to her every second night now. She didn't know how many times he had taken her.

During the days Washman left her pretty much to her own devices. They were on a high plateau deep in the highlands, and there were no roads to Washman's place. She had tried counting trees on their way up the mountain, after the highway ended. She had tried counting the ridges they crossed, the ravines they skirted, the streams they forded, the shale slides they gingerly picked their way over, but her knowledge of numbers was limited, and night fell, and the mule's rocking stride put her to sleep in the saddle long before they reached the homestead. She was held upright only by Washman's strong left arm.

Washman had told her she could go down into the lowlands if she wanted, but he would not help her. Then he had told her about the coyotes and what they would do to her if the pack caught her, and he had pointed out their doglike tracks in the dirt of the yard, dozens of trails that looped and crossed and recrossed the yard. He had shown her the tufts of clotted gray fur that lay on the ground in the mornings, and told her that the idiot animals pulled the hide off their brothers out of hunger and boredom and frustration, that they ate it and could not digest it and threw it up again. "They do that night after night out in the yard, and that's what you hear," he said.

She did not know what direction to take from the homestead, and the landscape of the plateau gave her no indication.

She had decided that she would leave within the next few days, while the moon was waxing, take her chances with the coyotes. She figured she would walk a line straight out from the door of the place and dead ahead as far as she could go. She would check the watch from time to time to see if it had come back to true rhythm again. She knew that the watch would tell her when she was clear of the place and its magnetic rocks, which distorted the flow of the days. When she had come to a place where the mechanism's pace came back to itself, that would be time enough to imagine a way back to people and a way to another kind of life. That would be time enough to imagine what that different life might be like.

Meanwhile, since the moon was a slim crescent in the sky and the nights were dark, she played the watch's tunes over and over again, and whistled them, and made words for them in her head. Each day she opened the watch and played the tunes, listened closely to the tinkling notes and checked them against the versions she had in her memory. Each day she was relieved to find that no notes had disappeared or reversed their order and that the songs replayed at the same tempo and in the same register that she remembered.

She could not bear the notion that their order might begin to vanish, but she had no assurance that it would not. She waited for the day when the songs wound themselves together into one meaningless filament of melody or, far simpler, stopped altogether.

Her dreams on the plateau were distorted and strange. She thought of Gandy as she went to sleep at night, and of the Italian who had come before Gandy, hoping to spur night visions of them. Always, though, she dreamed of some alien airless place where she choked and shrieked and her screams made no sound. The people of that bare atmosphere were like weak vain ghosts themselves: they drifted toward her and over her and sometimes through her as she choked, and the touch of them was cold. She woke from her dreams frightened and wearier than she had been when she lay down.

Grass did not grow near the homestead. Birds did not sing in the trees. The girl had seen a pair of sparrows flying overhead on her second day there, and she had followed their flight, chasing after them in her bare feet. She had found them, in the end, lying on a great escarpment of granite, and their bodies had been crisp and rigid. The birds lay on their backs with their scaled feet pointing to the sky.

No animals came near the house except the coyotes: no

deer, no raccoons, no bears drawn by the smell of food. The only animals she saw from day to day were Washman's livestock.

She turned from Washman, holding her watch, whistling one of its tunes, and she went from stall to stall in the small shed. "Cow," she said to Washman's skinny Guernsey. "Cow," she said to the Guernsey's calf, which sucked at her toes when she pushed them into its enclosure.

"Goats," she said, and the buck and his two does peered at her over the edge of the berth with their strange eyes, their necks extended.

"Mule," she said to the mule, and it nudged her with its long head. "No sugar," she told it, and she opened her hands and held them out for the mule to examine them. It scraped its dry lips across her palms.

Washman watched her slow promenade. She wore one of his work shirts belted loosely at the middle with a piece of baling twine, and it was gigantic on her. Her face had grown thin in her time on the mountain. He listened to her singing a nonsense song in her reedy voice, and he knew that she was nothing but a child.

She left the shed, trotted into a patch of sun in the yard, turned her face up into the light, opened her mouth like it was a clean, cool rain that she wanted to drink down. Her calves were slim and strong and elegant below the hem of the rough shirt, and Washman felt a mean desire for her begin to fill him.

"Come here," he said. His voice was rough. His hand where she had bitten him began to throb, and he flexed his fingers. The smallest would not bend; her teeth had cut through the muscles and tendons.

He had thought for a time that he would die from the

poison that had been in that bite. He had burned with a fever that he thought would char him, and the girl, and the house and the shed and the animals in the shed and the whole place. Then the fever had broken, and he had been surprised to find himself alive and the girl still at the homestead.

She was looking at him. He did not know what name to call her. She had not told him about being Gandy's Clementine, or what her Italian name was before that, or her given name, and she had not made up a new name for herself. "Come in here," he said. He gestured behind him with one of his canes. She stayed where she was.

Washman started toward her, swinging on his canes. When he was a couple of yards from her, she whirled and bolted. Washman was startled by her speed. She made for the brush at the edge of the yard, and he went after her, scrambling like a spider. The sinews in his shoulders creaked from the effort. The girl drew away from him.

She ducked to enter the brush, where he knew he would lose her. Washman stretched back his hand, hurled one of the heavy canes at her. It struck her across her narrow shoulders. Washman heard her teeth click together, and she dropped. The work shirt caught on a thornbush as she fell, and she hung suspended for a moment, her arms and head dangling. The cloth of the shirt split, and she thumped to the ground. The golden pocket watch slipped from her slack hand.

Carried forward by the momentum of his throw, Washman fell too. His second cane flew from his grip and skittered across the dirt of the yard away from him. With his hands he dragged himself to the girl's body. He clasped her ankles, pulled her against him.

He saw that she was still breathing, and he wrapped his hand around her slim throat. It fitted neatly. His thumb found the hollow beneath the shelf of her jaw, and his forefinger rested on the delicate column of her spine. He could feel the knot that his cane had raised, hot and wet with blood at the base of her skull. He pressed the heel of his hand against her windpipe and felt the springy flesh there begin to give. With his other hand he tore open the buttons on the work shirt.

When the girl was nude, he began to fumble with his own britches. He huddled over her, pressed her to him, breathing hard. Her eyes were closed, but the lids twitched, as though the orbs were jerking wildly from side to side beneath them.

He cried out and looked away from her face. Something moved between him and the sun, a great shadow, and the sudden darkness on his flesh made him cold. Washman wondered at the eclipse for a moment. Then he realized that the darkness was the silhouette of a man, and that he was no longer alone in the clearing with the girl.

The doctor's son put the muzzle of his revolver against the back of Washman's head. He took in the bulk of the man, the humped back and the shriveled naked legs, the rough pants bunched around his ankles. Washman held himself suspended over the body of the girl, waiting for the bullet. The doctor's son tapped the side of Washman's head with the barrel of the revolver. "Get up," he said. "Get up off of her."

There had been twelve men in the posse when it set out from Fort Terrance. Seven of them stood now in the dirt of Washman's yard as Washman released his hold on the girl.

Of the missing five, two had been buried deep in a rock slide that the careless hooves of their horses had started. Two more had been drowned with their mounts in the crossing of an unknown and unnamed rapid dark river. The last had been bitten again and again by a seven-foot diamondback rattle-snake that had coiled itself against his stomach and legs in his bedroll during one cold night's bivouac. His swollen body hung head down across his saddle, and the agonized expression on his dead face was something terrible to see.

One of the men fetched Washman's canes and handed them to him. Washman rose to his feet, clumsily rearranged his clothes. Another posse member wrapped the girl in a thick blanket and held her in his arms, clasped tight against his chest. He propped her small head against his shoulder.

The doctor's son kept his eyes on Washman.

"You boys surprised me," Washman said. "I don't ever get anybody through up here, so there was no way to expect you."

"This is him," the doctor's son said.

"Sure it's me," Washman said. "Old Washman. I live up here."

"He's been in my place," one of the men said. He was a shopkeeper. "Nothing else in the world looks like he does, I guess."

"I know you too," Washman said, and the shopkeeper blinked. He didn't want Washman talking to him. He didn't want Washman's recognition.

"I've bought from you," Washman said. It encouraged him that anyone in this rough-looking crew knew who he was. "Powder and lead and shot molds and flour and knives and molasses and cloth. We traded together."

The shopkeeper's mouth twisted down as with a bad taste, and he looked away.

"I bring in hides," Washman said. "Coyote and cata-mount. I brought you a big old black bear hide one time that I hadn't cured right and you didn't care for it, didn't want it,

did you? You said it stank and nobody'd buy such a thing."
He couldn't get the shopkeeper's eye back. "It never bothered
me none, but then I don't run a shop, do I?" Washman said.

The doctor's son gestured back over his shoulder, and the
other men went to their horses and took up thin cord to bind
Washman's hands and a heavy length of rope to hang him
with. The girl opened her eyes and looked at the posse over
the shoulder of the man who held her. When he realized that
she was awake, he said to her, "You don't want to see this,
honey. This isn't a thing for you to know." He tried to push
her head back down against his neck, but she resisted. "I'll
watch."

The doctor's son heard her. "Let her witness," he said.
"She's in this, so let her see how it finishes."

They picked a live oak at the edge of the yard with a good
straight limb about ten feet off the ground, and one of them
climbed into the tree and out onto the limb. He bounced on
it, gently at first to see if it would take his weight, and then
harder and harder until they were all confident that it would
serve its purpose.

They led Washman over to the tree. He didn't look up at
it. Instead he looked at the men of the posse, and he saw that
they were whiskered and grimy and hardened by their ordeal
on the mountain. He noted the corpse slung over the eighth
horse, and the way the heads of all of the horses drooped,
the way their purple tongues pushed through their teeth. They
were finished.

"Had you a good hard transit, didn't you?" Washman
said. He tried to sound cheerful as he said it.

None of them spoke to Washman as they went about their
tasks. The men lashed his wrists together behind him, and
they were not gentle as they pulled the restraints tight. Wash-

man swayed when they took his canes from him, and he would have fallen if two of the men had not seized him under his arms to hold him up. The doctor's son couldn't tell from the way Washman acted whether he knew what they were about or not. He wondered if Washman had it in his head that they were trussing him to haul him back to the valley.

"That's a fancy pistol you got," Washman said to the doctor's son, who thumbed back the hammer on the don's dragoon but said nothing in reply. Washman recognized the revolver—there could not be two in the country like it, he believed—and he was curious how the tall man with the cruel eyes had come to have it. He thought if he asked the question the man would probably put a bullet in him right then.

The men fashioned a noose from the thick rope. There were no executioners among them, and it took them awhile to make a working slip knot. They pulled it tight around one man's wrist and tugged at it, and when it didn't slide off they judged it sufficient for the job.

"I know I shouldn't have done that little girl the way I did," Washman said. He was addressing all of them now. The man who held the girl walked off a little ways into the woods and sat on a fallen log and rocked her back and forth. He sang a little song to her that he had sung to his own children when they were small and had a fever. He sat with his back to the yard and the house and the posse and all of it. The girl didn't take her eyes off Washman.

"It was just a thing that come over me," Washman said. "One minute she was like my daughter and the next she was like my wife, and I'd be awful hard put to tell you where the difference lay."

"This isn't about the girl," the doctor's son said.

"What is it, then?" Washman asked. "You look like a

crowd of desperadoes. There's little enough here, but you fellows take what you want, why don't you. Maybe you need you a little resupply."

"We're not bandits. We don't want anything from you," the doctor's son said. "You murdered a man down to the valley, and we're here to collect on that."

Washman's face clouded. "Murdered?" he said. Then his expression cleared. "Oh," he said. "The fop. You come all the way up here for him? There's no problem about that, then."

"You admit to it," the doctor's son said. "You killed him? We know you did, but we're interested to hear it from you. That's best."

"I don't care if we hear it from him," the shopkeeper said. A couple of the other men agreed.

"We come a long way. Men are dead over this. Now let's get on," the shopkeeper said.

"I killed him all right," Washman said. "But look, he shot me too. We shot each other." He tried to drag his shirt up to show them the chunk of flesh that the don's revolver had torn out of him, but his hands were tied. The men shifted toward him.

They forced Washman's head up and slipped the noose around his neck, which was as thick and strong as the rest of his torso, and deeply sunk between his massive shoulders. They tossed the free end of the rope over the tree limb, and three of them wrapped the rope around their hands and forearms and took the slack out of it.

Washman felt the pressure of the rope around his throat. "You want me to show you the way down the mountain," he said. "I guess you paid a high price getting up here, and it'll be just as high going down. You'll die, but it's a simple day's ride for me." He didn't say it like he was begging, but more like it was just a fact that he thought they ought to know.

"Bring over your horse," the doctor's son said to the shopkeeper.

"I don't want him on my horse," the shopkeeper said. "Ruins an animal forever, you hang a man off it. I'd have to walk down the mountain."

The doctor's son looked at the other men, and they stared back at him. They wouldn't volunteer their mounts, and none of them wanted to haul the dead man off his horse so they could use the animal in Washman's hanging.

The girl whispered to the man who held her. "What's that?" he asked her. She whispered to him again.

"What does she say?" the doctor's son asked him.

"She says, 'His mule is his legs,' " he said. "She says his mule can go anywhere she can go."

"What's that mean?" the shopkeeper asked.

"Is there a mule?" the doctor's son asked Washman. Washman just looked at him. One of the men went around Washman's house to the shed and returned in a minute, leading the mule by its rope halter.

"There's a cow in there, and goats," he said. The mule hauled back against the halter, stiffened its front legs, refused to cross the yard. The man hit at it with his open hand. "It tried to bite me when I put the halter on it," he said, and someone else in the group laughed. The laugh was brief and bitter.

"Hey, hey," Washman said to the mule, and it unlocked its legs, allowed itself to be led to him. "You jug," he said to it. He sounded happy to see the mule. "You splinter."

"I'm going to shoot it after we get done," the man said.

He and the shopkeeper stooped and boosted Washman onto the mule's back. They held him steady.

The doctor's son gestured at the men who held the rope. They took the new slack out of it. "Do what you want to me when we get down into the flatlands," Washman said. The men who held him up stepped away, and he sagged against the noose. They wrapped the rope around a nearby sapling, tied it tight.

The doctor's son pointed his revolver into the sky, pulled the trigger. The shot echoed in the clearing, but the mule wasn't frightened. It stood where it was. It snorted. "Just go easy," Washman said. "That's it."

The doctor's son holstered the revolver. He grabbed the mule's thick tail in his hands and twisted it into a tight spiral. He ground the tail hard into the mule's backside. The mule groaned and stepped away from the pain.

"Don't," Washman said as the mule walked out from under him. His thin legs trailed over the mule's rib cage, and its sharp hipbones bumped against his thighs. He rolled off its back altogether. The mule hobbled a dozen yards and stopped, facing away from Washman and the posse. It cropped at a little tuft of thistle that it had found.

The man who held the girl spoke in a choked voice. "Absalom met the servants of David," he said. "And Absalom rode upon a mule, and the mule went under the thick boughs of a great oak, and his head caught hold of the oak, and he was taken up between the heaven and earth, and the mule that was under him went away."

"What's that?" someone asked him.

"The Book of Samuel," he said.

"May God have mercy on your soul," the doctor's son said to Washman.

"Until you are dead dead dead," the shopkeeper said.

Washman's body bent like a bow as he battled against his bonds. The twine around his wrists groaned and cracked, and it ate deep into the flesh of his arms as he pitted his awesome strength against it. His body swung from side to side as he fought. The rope rubbed bark from the branch over his head, and the bark sprinkled him, caught in his hair, fell into his eyes. One of the men went to check the security of the knot at the sapling and found it solid.

Washman continued his struggle long after all the men had expected him to die. They looked at one another as he dangled before them. "This ain't going nowhere," one of them said. "His neck never broke when he come off the mule." He was one of the big men who had pinned the doctor to the ground outside the clinic the night Gandy Dolan died. His brother had disappeared screaming under a slide of wickedly pointed shale days before.

He went to where Washman was hanging and pulled hard on Washman's legs. Washman had no strength to knock him off. The man continued to pull, and after a minute one of the others joined him. They clung to Washman's legs and pulled and pulled. Finally they both climbed partway up his body, and they were all three hanging above the ground and swinging there when Washman's neck broke.

The posse ransacked the house and found Washman's gun and his rough clothes and all his traps, but none of it was of any value to them. They brought the cow and her calf from the shed with the idea of taking them down the mountain, and they butchered the two does to provision the trip. Then they set fire to the shed, and they left the buck inside to burn.

It had been a dry spring, and a light wind pushed the fire from the shed to the house, and from the house to the trees at the edge of the clearing. The trees caught quickly. Their sap boiled and they exploded around the posse like artillery shells. The men mounted their weary frantic horses and rode without direction or unity, trying to keep ahead of the wall of heat, and they were deathly afraid of the conflagration they had started.

Behind them the fire roared and hissed as it consumed the buildings and the animals and Washman's hanging body. The mule took a few faltering steps out of the clearing, its nostrils flaring, its eyes red with the glare. Then it stopped and turned to face the fire, which advanced with a predator's speed into the deep secret marrow of the forest.

Two days after Washman's hanging, while the people of Fort Terrance were still watching the hills for the red bloom of fire and the sky was dark with smoke, a man rode into town. He was bent nearly double over the pommel of his saddle. It was the man who had carried the girl away from the site of the hanging. She rode behind him on his horse, clutching the singed blanket around her. Their hair had burned away. Their eyes were red and running, their nostrils bloody, and they coughed a milky fluid. Their lungs strained at the clear air of the valley.

The man told his story to the people who helped him out of his saddle. He told them about the search for Washman's place. He told them about the hanging and the fire, and how the vegetation of the plateau had ignited around them. He did not know where the others were. He figured that they had died.

A few people wanted to head up into the hills, to find the bodies of those who had been washed away or buried or burned. Most favored leaving the dead to the dead. There were few enough people to undertake such a journey in any case. Those who would have been likeliest to try were those who had vanished.

The woman with the ruined arm sat on the porch of her house an hour or more before dawn, because her arm pained her and made it impossible to sleep. She had agreed to take the girl in and give her a home, and her house smelled of the girl's singed hair. The woman sat in a hard wooden chair and tried to find a position for her arm that would give her some ease.

She had found a way to sit, with the bad arm wrapped across her body and the hand gripping the opposite elbow, when she heard a car coming down the street. She stood, and the doctor's son drove past her place in his fancy automobile. In the dim light of pre-morning she strained her eyes to make out the figure behind the wheel, already knowing whose it was.

His hair had burned away, and his eyebrows, and his face was seared into an awful grin. His hands were horny, cooked claws on the steering wheel of the car. He had on the clothes he had worn when he left with the posse, and they were ragged with travel and foul with cinders. Threads of smoke curled up from the collar of his coat and the cuffs of his shirt sleeves. He did not look to the left or to the right of him, but only straight ahead.

She called out to him, but he seemed not to hear her. He turned at the crossroads at the edge of town and moved beyond her sight. She did not follow, and soon the noise of his car was gone too, and she knew that neither she nor anyone else would see him again.

From behind the porch's screen door, the girl said, "There goes another. There goes yours." She came onto the porch, took the woman's good hand into her own. Her hand was small and smooth.

"You saw him," the woman said. "I didn't know if he was there or just a thing that I imagined."

"I'm going to have a baby," the girl said.

The woman looked at her. Her face was so young, so narrow, that it was difficult to credit her words. "Whose?" she said.

"Hard to know," the girl said. "People will believe that it's Washman's. They'll call it Washman, and that will become its name."

"It's Gandy's," the woman said. "It might be Gandy Dolan's."

"It will be a monster. I'll be mother to a monster that has eyes but no other part of a face. The flames sang it to me when their curtain passed over. They took my hair but they left me alive."

She wept then, and the woman took the girl onto her lap and into her arms, though the movement sent waves of nausea sweeping through her. She hummed a little, a Chopin nocturne that she had once played on the piano, and the girl's slim body relaxed. The girl hummed along, and then she sang, in her small tuneless voice, a song with words of her own devising.

"Where did you learn that?" the woman asked. The girl opened her mouth to tell, but she fell into a dreamless sleep before she could speak even a word about the don's great golden pocket watch.

THE PANTHER

A BEDTIME STORY

The boy led his spavined horse through the dwarf brush that grew at the top of the mountain. The gelding's damaged leg was hot with pain, and he held its head close to him by its rope halter. He put his face against its warm brown neck and made soft comforting noises.

There were no roads; the boy followed vague trails that wandered among the trees and petered out and picked up again farther on. He wore a big-brimmed hat that he constantly pushed back from his forehead so he could see. He had a belt full of heavy brass cartridges slung over his shoulder. The cartridges fit the rifle that rode in a leather scabbard on the gelding's offside wither, and they also fit the Colt revolver cinched against the boy's ribs under his jacket.

He had lost the panther he was trailing in the morning of the day. The panther was an aged mountain cat, a hunter gone sheep-stealer. The boy spent the afternoon looking for his way down off the mountain and didn't find it. Now it was evening and he was searching for a clear space to lay out his bedroll, some green forage for the gelding among the sticker bushes and stunted trees. He took a drink from his canteen, wet the palm of his hand, held it against the muzzle of the gelding.

The horse nickered and stepped away from him, dancing on three good legs. The boy gripped the halter tight, reached over the gelding's neck, and unslung the rifle. He scanned the trees for the panther's form. The gelding shunted itself around in a wide half-circle, kicked at the brush, nipped the boy with its long yellow teeth. Hold up there, the boy said, trying to calm the horse. Hold up, he said again.

An old woman stepped from the woods onto the narrow path and pushed past the struggling boy and horse. The gelding struck out at her. I'm sorry, the boy said. He was trying to keep the gelding back from the old woman, and it was a hard job. The gelding was trying to climb right over him.

The old woman backed off a couple of steps, watching the two of them for a second. She was dressed all in greasy leathers, and she carried a battered iron stewpot in her hand. He's gone crazy, the boy said. He never did anything like this before with me. The gelding had tangled its tack in a thick gorse bush, and the boy dropped the rifle to try and pull it free. The old woman looked at the rifle and then headed down the path again.

Stand by a minute, the boy called after her. Is it a way down the mountain that you know of? The old woman vanished among the trees. The gelding stood shivering and blowing, still caught fast. It had torn its hide on the thorns as it fought, and the boy's hands were cut and bleeding. He worked to free it—reins, stirrups, mane, tail—and every time the gelding shifted, the boy gashed himself again. You, he said and slapped his fist against the gelding's dusty barrel side. You. The gelding held its lame foot tenderly off the ground, flared its nostrils.

The boy managed after a time to work the horse loose from the briers. He retrieved the rifle and set off down the path after the old woman. The gelding stumbled after him, stopping now and again to crop at the patches of thin yellow grass that grew along the edge of the path.

When it was full dark under the trees, the boy spied a light off to his left. As he approached, he saw the old woman sitting at her campfire in a little clearing. Her hair was wild and glowed orange in the light. The stewpot sat in the hot ashes at the edge of the fire, and the boy smelled lamb and onions and potatoes and pepper. He licked his lips. The gelding started to shy, and the boy tied the reins to a branch when he was still a dozen yards out of the clearing. Stand fast, he said to the gelding, and it pushed its broad head against his middle.

Hey granny, he said to the old woman as he walked into the camp. I'm sorry about the horse trying to bite back there, he said. He held out his arm, where a purple bruise was forming. He got me worse'n he did you, though, the boy said.

The old woman said to him, You got no rifle with you, son.

A man don't carry long-arms into a stranger's camp, the boy said.

You got good manners, the old woman said. Get you some eat.

The boy took the stewpot from the fire and set to, eating with a spoon and metal dish that he carried with him. The stew was hot and filling, and the lamb was cooked tender. The old woman rolled a cigarette and smoked and watched him while he ate.

Thankee, the boy said when he was finished. You live alone all the way up here, do you? he said.

I'll show you a thing, the old woman said. It's a thing nobody else has ever seen, and a thing you'll not see again. I show it to you 'cause you got good manners, and 'cause you brought no rifle into my camp, she said.

Okay, the boy said.

Then you follow the path down the mountain, the old woman said, and she pointed the way out to him. You take it straight down the mountain, straight into the valley. And no more hunting the panther, she said, 'cause it ain't what you think it is, and it's the last one of them left.

Okay, the boy said.

And don't you touch that belly gun you got, the old woman said, and she smiled. You ain't *too* polite.

That's my daddy's lamb there in that pot, ain't it? the boy said.

The old woman threw back her head and her eyes rolled in their sockets. She fell to the ground and writhed in the dirt of the clearing floor, and her body shucked its uncured leathers. The boy touched the revolver at his waist, but the feel of it was foreign to the scene before him and he did not draw the gun.

Something rose on the far side of the fire, and it wasn't the old woman there anymore but the giant catamount. Its great head was blunt, its eyes dark as key slots. Its long narrow body was covered with terrible scars. Some, the boy knew, he had inflicted, and his father and his family and those that peopled the valley. Others were the claw-work of beasts. Still others he imagined were the marks of the darts and spears of ancient savages.

The panther circled the boy, and he thought how he would tell his children and perhaps his grandchildren about the gray-yellow color of that hide and the puckers and tucks in the flesh and of the animal reek that suddenly hung in the air of the clearing.

The panther leapt the fire, and the boy blinked in fear as it stood over him. He could feel its breath on him and hear the beat of its weary heart. Then it leapt again, and though he strove to watch, he did not know if the cat rushed along the ground or hurtled into the boughs of a tree or even if it sped upward and outward and vanished into the clear night sky.

THE ELECTRIC GIRL

A RADIO PLAY

CHARACTERS:

MURPHY

LILLY

MR. COTTON

THE BARKER

CHARLIE CHARLIE

THE ELECTRIC GIRL

MURPHY: What you got to know is, she died of her own faults and decision-making, Lilly. She died of vanity, is what really killed her.

LILLY: Vanity never killed her. You rolled the car into the reservoir and you let her drown.

MURPHY: I absolve myself of the responsibility. Even the cops said there wasn't nothing I could of done to help.

LILLY: They charged you with manslaughter, Murphy.

MURPHY: Involuntary manslaughter. That means you got no real choice in the matter but just surrendered yourself up to circumstances.

LILLY: Still, manslaughter, after all. That's a terrible thing.

MURPHY: The jury knew I didn't have nothing to do with it. They could see it in my eyes that I had no fault, and I could see it in their eyes that they wouldn't ever convict.

LILLY: You told me all this before. It was a long time ago. I don't want to hear it anymore.

MURPHY: I sincerely believe that idea, that you can see a thing in a person's eyes. I could tell you what's inside you.

LILLY: No you couldn't. I don't like that kind of game.

MURPHY: Hold still, let me get a look at you. Pull that lamp over a little. It needs a clear light to reveal someone's intention.

LILLY: Don't come close. I don't want you so close to me like that.

MURPHY: You used to not mind it.

LILLY: I used to not mind any number of things that I can think of. I used to not mind heat and bugs in the summer either.

MURPHY: It's okay anyhow. I seen what I was after.

LILLY: You seen me leaving. You seen me getting out of here in just a minute. That's what's in there.

MURPHY: I seen you trying to leave. No success in that plan, though. It was all defeat and resignation on that point.

LILLY: You never seen nothing like that.

MURPHY: And I seen your love for me. It was all folded up like a package. It was neglected but whole.

LILLY: There's nothing for you. Nothing about you. It's just about me and getting out.

MURPHY: You'll never do it. I'd kill you before it came to that. I'd find some way to stop your plan.

LILLY: You just watch me do it. Use your eyes that see. Just let me get my stuff.

MURPHY: Go ahead and try it if you want. There's a force that will keep you from going.

LILLY: A force?

MURPHY: And that force is me.

LILLY: Get out of my way.

MURPHY: Where is it you want to go?

LILLY: I got places. I got a place to go.

MURPHY: You got a man. Some people said you was seen with an Indian-looking guy a while ago, but I didn't believe it. Big Indian.

LILLY: That's him. That's Charlie Charlie.

MURPHY: I heard you was kissing him. They said you was necking in a public place. They said you appeared to be satisfied.

LILLY: I'm proud to kiss him wherever we may be. He asked me to come and live with him to be like his wife.

MURPHY: You don't want him. What is it you want him for? You got me.

LILLY: He'll take you apart stone by stone if you don't let me be. He knows a bunch of violent tricks that he won't hesitate to use. Watch out.

MURPHY: I've been known to grow violent myself sometimes.

LILLY: You do nothing. Involuntary manslaughter is the best you can do. Don't tell me.

MURPHY: You don't mean that. That was no violence on my part. A lack of initiative is all you can get me for there. I explained what happened.

LILLY: I don't care about it. The girl's dead, so just leave her dead.

MURPHY: She had her window closed is why she died. She had beautiful long red hair and she didn't want the wind and the dust to get in it. She had no way out of the car.

LILLY: You were drunk. You're drunk now.

MURPHY: We had a fight one time, me and her. I was violent that time. I had my hands on her throat to choke her and she just looked at me with these calm green eyes. Aqua eyes. That took all the fight out of me, the way she looked then.

Lilly's *footsteps recede as she walks into an adjoining room.*

Lilly: (*calling out*) What did she look like dead?

Murphy: I had the window down on my side. It cooled me when it was hot. I liked the way the breeze came in and made it feel like we were going fast. She managed to get one hand around my ankle when I went out the window.

Lilly: I'm leaving the bridesmaid dress. Charlie Charlie's got him some land, and we're going to start up a horse farm. Won't need a dress like that out there.

Murphy: I thought she wasn't ever going to let go of that ankle. I was half in and half out of the window, and under the water it was cold and gray and full of floating things. I kicked her off, if the truth be told.

Lilly: The shoes with the heels, too. Maybe whoever comes along after a while will want them. They go with the dress.

Murphy: She had my shoe in her hand when they pulled her out of the water. Her hair had turned green, like verdigris copper, in the time she was down there. Her eyes were wide in terror and the recognition of death.

Lilly: Like Charlie Charlie did for me. Really you ought to be happy for me.

Murphy: You aren't leaving, Lilly. Put all that stuff back in there.

Lilly's *footsteps approach as she reenters the room where* Murphy *is.*

LILLY: I think I got everything. Anything I might of forgotten you can have.

A cabinet opens and a heavy object is withdrawn.

MURPHY: I got a gun. It's got shells in it. It's your death I hold here in my hand.

He works the slide of a pump shotgun.

MURPHY: You'll be killing yourself if you try to go.

LILLY: Murder ain't in you, Murphy. Get out of my way.

MURPHY: Kiss me. Be kind to me. You were kind to me in the past when I needed it.

LILLY: You know I'm not about to kiss you. You're making everything worse than it is.

MURPHY: Kiss me before you go and I'll let you out of here.

LILLY: Charlie Charlie will carve you up for meat patties if I tell him you did like this with me. Don't make me mad. He does what I want him to.

MURPHY: I do what you want me to. I won't shoot. But you got to kiss me first. Once like you mean it. I'm giving you that chance.

LILLY: Those days are gone for good.

MURPHY: Just a little one, then. Nothing so serious. Just touch me on the lips.

LILLY: I'm done kissing you. I'm done touching you in every way.

MURPHY: Then I have to shoot you.

LILLY: Kill me or let me pass.

MURPHY: You'll die.

LILLY: Goodbye, Murphy.

LILLY *takes a couple of steps.* MURPHY *shoots her. After a couple of silent seconds, a telephone begins to ring. Throughout the following conversation, MR. COTTON's voice is filtered by a poor telephone connection.*

MR. COTTON: (*answering the phone*) Hello?

MURPHY: *sighs, takes a deep breath.*

MR. COTTON: Hello? Hello?

MURPHY: I . . .

MR. COTTON: I know you're there because I can hear you. I don't like this type of phone call. I have to go if you don't say something.

MURPHY: Mr. Cotton, this is Murphy. Murphy Johnson.

MR. COTTON: Who's that?

MURPHY: I live with your girl. Lilly's my girlfriend.

MR. COTTON: I don't know you.

MURPHY: We never met.

MR. COTTON: I didn't want to. There's something twisted inside you that drew Lilly on. I knew it when she talked about you. She's like that.

MURPHY: Yes.

MR. COTTON: She loves the darkness that resides in men. It

pulls at her like her own special gravity. Her personal history is full of beatings and small wickedness.

MURPHY: Yes.

MR. COTTON: So I didn't want to meet you. You were nothing different.

MURPHY: I've shot her, Mr. Cotton. I killed her.

MR. COTTON: Are you drunk?

MURPHY: Yes sir.

MR. COTTON: Were you drunk when you did it to her?

MURPHY: Yes sir. I mean, it was the same drunk. I'm still drunk. It wasn't very long ago.

MR. COTTON: You are selfish and stupid. You are a selfish, selfish man.

MURPHY: Don't I know it. The evidence is right here before me. It's something I wish I had never done.

MR. COTTON: Lilly's there with you now, you say. Are you sure she's dead?

MURPHY: It's a fact.

MR. COTTON: You stabbed her to death. Or did you choke her? Grab her neck and wring it?

MURPHY: I shot her. I told you before. It's a terrible sight. I can't bear to describe it to you.

MR. COTTON: You better not. None of me wants to hear it, not a single part of me.

MURPHY: I didn't even touch her and I got blood on me. The blast hurled her back at a terrific rate.

MR. COTTON: Did she cry? Did my baby scream, there at the end?

MURPHY: She didn't make a sound.

MR. COTTON: I expect the police are on their way to get you.

MURPHY: I don't think so. I didn't call them.

MR. COTTON: You want to hang up the phone then. You want to call them and tell them about the thing that you did.

MURPHY: I can't tell what to do yet. I have to consider my course of action for a while. I don't want to get shot. I don't want some kind of accident to happen where I might get killed or hurt bad.

MR. COTTON: I'll call them on you. I'll tell them about Lilly and we'll see what they do to you.

MURPHY: You don't know where I am.

MR. COTTON: I know your name. That's enough. They got all kinds of computers and whatnot these days that'll look for you.

MURPHY: I won't be here when they come.

MR. COTTON: They'll put your likeness around. You'll be a hunted man, and then they'll catch you.

MURPHY: I don't know if you know my name or not, anyway. I said it, but I bet you don't remember.

MR. COTTON: I do.

MURPHY: What is it, then?

MR. COTTON: Dunphy.

MURPHY: No.

MR. COTTON: Thompson.

MURPHY: That ain't it either.

MR. COTTON: I'm not playing with you. My daughter is dead. You did it and you're standing over her body now and you got to pay the price. I imagine even a twisted piece of work like you must see that.

MURPHY: I know it. I don't plan to evade justice forever. I've just got to have some time. I need to figure a couple of things out.

MR. COTTON: Why are you speaking to me? I don't have an interest in your plans.

MURPHY: Lilly talked some about you. She told me some of the things you've done in your life. She said you were a preacher or something.

MR. COTTON: I served the Lord in my time. I spread His word. I lived a righteous life. I knew His intention for me, and I dared carry it out to the best of my ability.

MURPHY: I owe you an explanation. I figure I'll come up there. I'll see you. Between you and me we can work something out.

MR. COTTON: No.

MURPHY: It'll take me about a couple of hours to show up there. I got the stain on me. I need you to help get it off. I need to wash it off me.

MR. COTTON: Don't come here. I won't honor your presence. I'll have the police waiting on you. I'll shoot you down like a dog myself.

MURPHY: You will?

MR. COTTON: I'll break your bones with rocks. I'll shatter your teeth and pluck your eyes out of their sockets. I'll drive the breath from your lungs. I'll make sure that you're punished.

MURPHY: I better not come up there.

MR. COTTON: You better not.

MURPHY: Okay. If you feel like that.

MR. COTTON: You wouldn't survive it.

MURPHY: No. I ought to go. I ought to hang up now.

MR. COTTON: I want your blood for what you done. There's no help I can give you.

MURPHY: I'll let you know how it all comes out.

MR. COTTON: Don't you ever call here again.

MURPHY: Okay. Goodbye.

MR. COTTON: I won't say goodbye to someone like you. I won't even do that for you.

MURPHY: I understand. I got you. Goodbye, Mr. Cotton.

MURPHY *hangs up. The closed phone line hums. The sound fades, to be replaced after a couple of silent seconds by the sounds of a carnival midway, continuing.*

BARKER: Born of a woman, born to live, born to grow and thrive in a world they never made. We got 'em here, we got 'em now. Alive, alive, alive. This is the tent, this is the show. It's live, it's continuous, it's fifty cents. Talk to 'em, watch 'em breathe, just don't you dare pass 'em by. And these are the freaks we got: we got the two-headed man, the monkey girl, the lizard girl, the untamed Borneo jungle boy, the vicious and uncivilized chicken-gobbling geek. It's not a fake, it's not an illusion. We got the quarter-man, gone from the diaphragm down, walks on his hands; the amazing pinhead. There's the little fire-eating dwarf, tiny enough that you could flush him down the toilet if he should give you cause. See the lovely electrical girl, but don't touch her no matter how much she begs you to; there's fifty thousand eye-popping volts in that lovely, barely clad she-male form. She's a vast capacitor made of flesh. She can light a fluorescent bulb or jump-start a diesel truck with just her delicate hands, but her caress has killed a dozen men. It's all here, it's all alive, alive, alive, and it's all for fifty, fifty, fifty cents.

MURPHY: Hey. You, the freak show guy.

BARKER: If you got fifty cents you can go on in, buddy. See it all, take it in. You'll never think the same way about your human form again.

MURPHY: You got a fortune-teller in there? You got somebody that reads the future and tells it to you? That's what I come down for, if you got it.

BARKER: No fortune-teller. Gypsy's next tent over, but she's a gyp, get it? We got the real thing. We got the two-headed man, monkey girl, elephant-skin girl.

MURPHY: What could make a person like that? It's a trick. How come they're like that?

BARKER: Who can say? I got no direct knowledge. Born of a woman, born to live. That's them. Go on in and see it for yourself. You'll see it's no kind of a trick.

MURPHY: Something they did? I bet it was a sin or a crime in their past that got them transformed. It caught up with them and here they are.

BARKER: Okay, buddy. I'll tell you: sins of the mother visited upon the next generation. Every one of them. Monkey girl's mother fornicated with a lower order of primate, okay? I hate to tell it, I don't often do it, but you seem to want to know.

MURPHY: It's not their fault, then. They got to labor under somebody else's yoke.

BARKER: Unfair as hell, but there it is. Pinhead's mother married her brother, a hard-drinking, rock-fisted logger, strong and sexy as hell. She couldn't resist him. The quarter-man's mother took thalidomide. Electric girl's mother stood out in a rainstorm and cursed the God that made her. Lightning stroke turned her to a smoking deanimated shell but left the little baby fetus alive in the carbonized womb, doomed to live life without the press of flesh against her, doomed to kill whatever she loves. Do you like that?

MURPHY: It tears at me. I wish I was still ignorant.

BARKER: There you go. That's what we're here for.

MURPHY: I better head out.

BARKER: No, stick around. I made all that up. I wanted to see what you thought. I wanted to see if it enhanced your appreciation any.

MURPHY: I got problems of my own. I come down here for a fortune-teller. It was all I could think of.

BARKER: Mind you, it might as well be true. Hell, by tomorrow they'll be telling it that way to each other. I tell them their lives and they believe it.

MURPHY: You've got a persuasive tone.

BARKER: Without me, the freaks are just ugly. They scare off people like you. With me, they got romance, they got dash.

MURPHY: See you after a while. Maybe I'll come in after I consult with the gypsy.

BARKER: Whoa there, wait up. You can't go over there. She's a fake. She's got nothing for you.

MURPHY: I done a thing I got to tell her about. Maybe she can read in the cards and give me the idea for a plan.

BARKER: You did something. What did you do? You killed somebody.

MURPHY: Yes.

BARKER: You did? I just made that up. That came right off the top of my head.

MURPHY: I killed her all right. You didn't make it up. I wish you did.

BARKER: Wife? Girlfriend?

MURPHY: Lilly was my girl. I loved her like I was out of my mind, and I shot her before I knew I was going to do it.

BARKER: She didn't love you anymore, right? She was on her way out and you just figured to stop her, I bet.

MURPHY: That's a keen head on your shoulders.

BARKER: I heard stories like it before. It's not the first one anybody ever told me. Not by a long shot.

MURPHY: What did they do? The other folks that told you their story.

BARKER: Went to jail, mostly. Some took their own life. One even paid me a hundred dollars to arrange for him to make love with the electric girl. It was a desperate last act.

MURPHY: I wouldn't want to end up that way.

BARKER: You should of seen him. Every hair was standing up on his body and head, and there was live steam coming out of his nostrils and mouth. He was like a piece of toast.

MURPHY: What did the electric girl do?

BARKER: She just laughed a little is all. She knew it would happen to him. She's seen it before. She cried a little too.

MURPHY: That ain't the thing for me. There's things in my life left undone.

BARKER: You got to get a feeling of completion about what you done. You got to have a method for clearing up what you skewed so bad.

MURPHY: That's the thing in the world I lack most at this point.

BARKER: A murderer incurs a number of debts in the commission of his act, I guess.

MURPHY: Don't I know it. I felt the burden settle itself on my shoulders the minute I seen her hit the floor.

BARKER: You got to square yourself with the people you wronged. That's Plan A. Take it from me. Then you got to live a different life than the one you been leading. You got to change the attitude you have for the world and become a benefit to your fellow man. That's Plan B.

MURPHY: I tried. I already tried and failed.

BARKER: What did you try?

MURPHY: Her old man is crazy and won't listen to anything I say to him when I try and explain. He just wants to kill me is all he wants. He ain't seen her for five, six years, but he acts like she was still his and lived under his roof.

BARKER: Still, a father's a father. You know he's got to hate you for what you done.

MURPHY: So there's nothing I can undertake on that score.

BARKER: Anybody else that you took her out of their life?

MURPHY: No. He's her only family that I know of. She had

her an Indian that she loved and he loved her. But I don't know what I might owe to that son of a gun.

BARKER: An Indian? What kind of an Indian?

MURPHY: I don't have the least idea. How many kinds are there? A big Indian.

BARKER: He might never know what happened. He might wonder forever about the events that took her life.

MURPHY: Had him a double name. Charlie Charlie is what it was.

BARKER: I wouldn't want to live like that, even for a single day. Wake up and call out for the one you love and get no answer back. Live with the mystery all the time, muddying up the waters in everything you do.

MURPHY: I don't know what I can do. I wouldn't know him if I saw him.

BARKER: Charlie Charlie, did you say? Shoot, I know that boy. I can't believe you iced Charlie Charlie's woman.

MURPHY: She was my woman.

BARKER: Big Indian is right. Charlie Charlie works the high steel in the city when there's work. He works out here as a carnie sometimes when there isn't. I seen him wrestle the fighting bear they got out here and win. He'll do it for five dollars.

MURPHY: When was it, the last time that you saw him?

BARKER: He helped to build that steel bridge they got not far from here. He watched men plunge into the gorge to their death, but they couldn't get him to wear a safety line. He walked them narrow beams like he was headed to the bathroom for a drink of water. He loved a high wind.

MURPHY: I never heard much about him before this.

BARKER: He's a regular celebrity out here. He's likely to exact a high price for what you done. There is a rumor of cannibalism in his family's history, and unconfirmed tales of other, darker crimes.

MURPHY: He seemed like the least of my worries when I did it. It was like he wasn't real to me at all. I never thought of him once.

BARKER: He'll look plenty real to you when you meet him. I don't envy you. Still, it's something you got to do.

MURPHY: I have my doubts.

BARKER: Sure, you got to see him. You know it. He'll hunt for you otherwise. He's a tracker. He'll be like a shadow behind you all the time. You don't want that.

MURPHY: I guess not.

BARKER: I guess you don't.

MURPHY: Where do I find him at?

BARKER: Don't sweat it. You come back here tonight, maybe one, two o'clock. The place will be all shut down. Just come on in the tent. I'll get Charlie Charlie for you. You're somebody he's going to want to meet.

MURPHY: You'll take care of it.

BARKER: You'll thank me.

MURPHY: It'll clear my mind.

BARKER: You be careful. Stay away from the hands of the authorities. They'll be looking for you about now, I bet.

MURPHY: I got a place I can go till then. I'll come back here tonight.

BARKER: You bet you will. I got to get back to work. I got a show tent full of freaks to fill up.

The carnival noise swells.

BARKER: (*shouting*) Born of a woman, born to live, born into a world they never made . . .

The BARKER *and the carnival noise fade together into silence. The following scene should sound as though it takes place under a great empty show tent.*

MURPHY: Hello? Anybody in here?

CHARLIE CHARLIE: Dark under here, ain't it?

MURPHY: Charlie Charlie?

CHARLIE CHARLIE: Hot, too. It never does seem to cool off in these big tents. Canvas just holds the hot air of the day in for a long time, like it was one of those big flying balloons or something.

MURPHY: I see you now. It took my eyes a couple of seconds to adjust is all.

CHARLIE CHARLIE: The kind of balloon with the little basket that hangs down underneath. They pull a chain and fill the balloon up with a big blue propane flame. The burner makes a hell of a racket when it goes off, and you can feel the balloon pull up under you right away, like it's a live thing.

MURPHY: I never been in one of those balloons.

CHARLIE CHARLIE: I been. I was just a little boy and my father took me. The basket sways under your feet from the winds a thousand feet up. It's an uncertain feeling. You can see the ground spread out beneath you like a giant blanket and pick out the place where you would land if you were to fall. It's an experience that can unsettle the lesser kind of man.

MURPHY: Did it scare you?

CHARLIE CHARLIE: I wasn't worried. It scared my father, though. I just wanted to climb up into the balloon itself. It was red and full and firm with the heated air. It had some kind of advertising slogan on the side. The pilot wouldn't let me up in the bag. He said the heat and the poisonous gases would kill me.

MURPHY: That's a very interesting story to me. I find that interesting. It's the kind of experience I've never had at all.

CHARLIE CHARLIE: What a body she had. Where did you shoot her?

MURPHY: What?

CHARLIE CHARLIE: Lilly. Where did you shoot her?

MURPHY: You mean the place where, or where on her person?

CHARLIE CHARLIE: The latter.

MURPHY: I used a twelve-gauge. The effect was pretty general.

CHARLIE CHARLIE: And now you want to apologize to me.

MURPHY: I guess so, yeah. As much as anything else. Before I go to live a different kind of life.

CHARLIE CHARLIE: I like that. That's good.

MURPHY: I thought it might be the thing to give us both a little peace. The barker said that I shouldn't leave you in a state of mystery.

CHARLIE CHARLIE: I would of hated it if you had done that.

MURPHY: I figured you would. The barker struck me as being a pretty sharp individual.

CHARLIE CHARLIE: Sharp.

Metal on leather: the sound of a knife being withdrawn from its sheath.

CHARLIE CHARLIE: It's good that you got in touch with me, Murphy. I can help you with that tortured conscience you got.

MURPHY: What is it you plan to do with that knife?

CHARLIE CHARLIE: Anything I want, that's what. Like it? Twelve inches of blade. They call it a bowie knife. It's named for Jim Bowie, a guy that died at the Alamo.

MURPHY: I heard of him.

CHARLIE CHARLIE: Most everybody has. He was a friend of Davy Crockett.

MURPHY: I come unarmed, Charlie Charlie. I didn't want nothing bad out of this meeting.

CHARLIE CHARLIE: I can throw this knife like an expert. I could have split your head the minute you came in if I wanted.

MURPHY: I'm glad you didn't do it.

CHARLIE CHARLIE: I'm like a magician when I get my hands on a knife. My whole family's like that.

MURPHY: It's a nice talent to have.

CHARLIE CHARLIE: Stick out your tongue for me, Murphy.

MURPHY: Why would you want me to do that?

CHARLIE CHARLIE: Because I'm tired of your talking. I want you to be quiet for a while. Stick it out and let me get ahold of it. I've got a couple of things I want to tell you about, and I don't need your interruptions.

MURPHY: I'll shut up. I'm happy to do that for you.

CHARLIE CHARLIE: Recall that I got this blade in my hands and I can kill you where you stand. There's no hesitation in me on that score, if you were wondering. Just give me your tongue.

MURPHY: Okay. You got it. I'm just trying to avoid a problem with you.

CHARLIE CHARLIE: Let me get a good grip on it. I'll try not to pull too hard.

MURPHY: (*slurred, as his speech remains*) Don't hurt me.

CHARLIE CHARLIE: I won't hurt you. Here, sit, you'll be more comfortable.

A *chair creaks.*

CHARLIE CHARLIE: I want to tell you some about me. I want you to understand things before you go on to live the different kind of life you been talking about. You got a slippery tongue, Murphy. Try not to move it around so much and I won't have to grip hard, okay?

MURPHY: Okay.

CHARLIE CHARLIE: I get a picture in my head. I get a clear image of what it is you did to her. It's like a vision. I see myself walking into the room where Lilly lays on the floor. I see myself picking through the objects around the room that are covered with blood: a busted picture frame, a vase, a hairbrush, a lamp that's a little ceramic man with his hunting dog.

MURPHY: There ain't—

CHARLIE CHARLIE: Hush. I take up the brush, and I run it through her lustrous hair, which looks just like when she was alive. It looks no different. And I run the brush through my hair too. That's my ceremony. That's how I say goodbye. And it's okay.

MURPHY: Ouch.

CHARLIE CHARLIE: Sorry. I didn't mean to pull so hard. It's okay, Murphy, because I got a certain object with me. I'm carrying it in my shirt pocket. That object is magical to me, it's like an amulet. It's completely mystical. And do you know what the object is?

Murphy: Don't.

Charlie Charlie: It's your tongue, Murphy. Of course you know that. You must have had the vision too.

Charlie Charlie *cuts out* Murphy's *tongue.* Murphy *shrieks tonguelessly, begins to cry.*

Charlie Charlie: I got it. All gone, Murphy. We're square now. I got what I need.

Charlie Charlie's *footsteps recede. The* Electric Girl's *lighter tread advances.*

Electric Girl: Hey. The barker said you wanted to see me. Lots of guys want to see me. But only once. (*She pauses.*) It can't be that bad. Don't you think I'm pretty? Lots of guys think I'm pretty. They tell me so. It's a thing that I like to hear. I'll turn all the way around if you like, so you can get a good look at me.

A low-grade buzz, continuing under.

Electric Girl: Hey baby, stop crying. Let me take a look at you. Let me see.

The buzz swells, crackles, continuing.

Electric Girl: Jeez, lookit the blood. How did you get all of that? What on earth have you been into?

Clothing rustles.

Electric Girl: I see. I understand. I know what you need. You sit there a minute. You just hold still. I'll take care of you.

The buzz crescendos. The chair creaks frantically, rhythmically. Murphy *wails.*

122

THE ELECTRIC GIRL

ELECTRIC GIRL: Hold me, hold me, hold me.

The buzz ceases. There is complete silence.

ELECTRIC GIRL: (*laughs, then sighs*) Jeez, willya lookit? What a mess. Cripes.

AT THE
ALHAMBRA

Johnnie and Anne sit out on the patio of the Hotel Alhambra in the morning sun, watching a holy procession out in the plaza. A man in the caravan stumbles as he passes them. He's supporting one corner of an eight-foot-tall image of the Madonna, which totters, sways sideways, is righted. It is covered in bright flowers, and some of them fall to the ground.

The procession circles the octagonal wooden bandstand in the center of the plaza. Beggars sleep in the bandstand at night. A brass orchestra occupies the place now, pumping out slow, solemn religious airs.

Anne thinks Johnnie is beautiful in his white shirt with the short sleeves, his forearms muscular and brown with the sun of the place. A Panama hat, a planter's hat, sits on the table near him. He said to her when he found it in the open-air market at Masaya, "They make these down here. This is

125

the place to get a hat like this one." Though they are in Nicaragua, not Panama.

It is 1970, and troops of the Guardia Civil occupy the intersections of most city streets. Anne does not like the way they eye her, pretty *norteamericana*, when she takes a walk. They wear carbines slung on canvas thongs over their shoulders. Their uniforms are in good shape, new, but the creases are dull in the humid air. Johnnie doesn't respect them as soldiers. He is an Air Force captain—was, until recently. He's a civilian now.

"This week is Holy Week," Anne says to Johnnie, who taps the tabletop in time with the footsteps of the pilgrims out in the plaza. "At home they're boiling eggs to dye. They're buying little chocolate rabbits wrapped in foil."

"Right," he says.

"You're drunk," she says.

"Right," he says. "Quite a country," he says. "Quite a little country. We should stay here. A man could live his life right here."

"I won't talk to you when you're drunk," she says. "Not when you're drunk in the morning."

"Get drunk in the morning, and still you stay in the best rooms in the best hotel in the whole damn country. Why don't we just live down here the rest of our lives, Annie? We should stay here. We should recognize a good thing."

"I won't have that conversation with you," she says. She turns from him. Her silence is not angry. It's almost companionable. She's pretty sure that Johnnie doesn't mean what he says, that he sees Granada is a small, sad city, Nicaragua is hot and dirty and poor. He knows about the earthquakes that tear apart the country, the active volcanoes that ring it.

He's talked about staying in every place they've seen on

their trip. He talked about it in Tampico, where they passed through Mexican customs, and in Vera Cruz, where they swam in the Gulf of Mexico, and in Tapachula, where slim Mexican girls lounged around the lighted pool at the Camino Real. He always loses the thread of the idea in the middle of the day, when the city around them dozes in the heat. Johnnie can't bear a siesta.

They'll go home in a couple of days, a week. Just get in the single-engine Cessna 172, tail number November 4743 Echo, blue metal bird, and head up the Pacific coast, across the isthmus of Mexico, back to the States. This is their vacation.

The Cessna waits at its tie-down at the new airport to the north, outside of Managua. Johnnie has said several times that he needs to take a ride up there, check the plane, make sure nobody's lifting parts for the black market, but he hasn't done it. They haven't left Granada in the week since they arrived.

"Isn't there another Alhambra somewhere?" Johnnie asks. "Isn't it a famous tomb or something?"

A column of children stalk past the hotel. They've got their own crude images: Mary and the baby Jesus, and other figures, Anne can't tell exactly who they are. Some of the Apostles, maybe, or the Wise Men. One of the icons, wrapped in white muslin, is clearly an angel, an archangel. These statues are sized down and gaily painted. Anne thinks that the children must have made them. The kids chatter and walk in a disorderly way, so that their statues bump and clack together. The brass band has dispersed.

"You haven't worn your hair back like that in a while," Johnnie says. Anne has her hair in a ponytail. She is wearing a pale yellow sundress. "I like it."

Johnnie's hair is cropped short, and he wears a pair of dark aviator glasses. He is clean-shaven, and his nose is long and thin and fine. There is a light sheen of sweat along his upper lip.

"It's dirty," she says. "I can't get the shampoo to foam up at all here. The water."

"It's awful," he says, and he takes a drink: Flor de Caña rum, which is local, and Pepsi-Cola. Anne drinks something called *limonada dulce*, which turned out not to be lemonade as she expected, but made from limes instead.

"Makes you look young, your hair that way," Johnnie says.

He has the aviator glasses on because the sun hurts his eyes, which are pale blue and can't stand intense light. They are the only weak part of him. The flesh around his eyes is dark and webbed and loose from the days of constant drinking. His hands rest flat on the table in front of him. When he takes a drink, they are steady. She wonders again when they are going to leave. Johnnie got them down and he'll get them back, she thinks. He is an excellent pilot.

The *limonada* has a bright bitter flavor, like the terminals of a dry cell, and to Anne it tastes clean. She tried chocolate milk when they first got to the Alhambra, but the milk was boiled, and the thin dead taste of it disgusted her.

"Where's the other Alhambra?" Johnnie says. Anne turns back to him, to tell him that he's asked before and that she doesn't have any idea. He's talking to *la señora*, though, the woman who owns the place. *La señora* has emerged from the kitchen with food for them: a plate of cold shrimp salad for Anne, and a plate of *huevos rancheros* for Johnnie. *La señora* always wears bedroom slippers, and she is silent when she walks, although she's very fat.

"The famous one," Johnnie says. "The one that's more famous than this." There's a joke in his tone, which *la señora* doesn't seem to get. She's an elderly Italian woman with her hair dyed freakish black and cut short. Everyone calls her *la señora*. She moved to Granada in the early sixties with *el señor*, she has told them. They bought the Alhambra sight unseen while they were still in Italy. They used their life savings to do it.

El señor is dying in a room in the owner's quarters of the hotel. Johnnie and Anne haven't met him, don't know what he's dying from. The doctor has told *la señora* that *el señor*'s life could be saved by the installation of a window air conditioner in his room. *La señora* has repeated this intelligence to Johnnie and Anne a couple of times. There's none to be had, she says, holding her hands out, palms up. Nowhere. Not at any price.

"As if she thought we brought one down with us," Anne has said to Johnnie, in their room, in the hot dark. "As if we had one on us."

Now *la señora* hands the shrimp salad to Anne without looking at her, lays Johnnie's plate before him. She casts a couple of forks out on the tabletop. Anne takes one for herself and surreptitiously wipes it with her handkerchief. She is sure they're only indifferently cleaned.

"The Alhambra," *la señora* says, "is a palace in Spain. It is built in Granada when the Moors swept across all of the continent in their resplendent armies. A caliph lives there."

"A caliph?" Johnnie says. He pauses with a forkful of eggs partway to his mouth.

"Lived there," Anne says. *La señora* is capricious in her use of English tenses. "I imagine it's used for something else now."

"Sure," Johnnie says. He's well into the plate of eggs already, and the spiciness of the food doesn't slow him down. The skin of his face has a slight reddish cast to it, but that's the only sign that he's affected at all.

Johnnie asks *la señora* for another drink—he wants beer this time, gropes for the word, comes up with *cerveza*—and she moves off into the kitchen to get it for him. Anne watches her go. She notes the sweat stain between *la señora*'s wide shoulders, and the way her linen dress is splitting there.

"I don't much care for her," Anne says.

"She's all right," Johnnie says. "She takes care of us okay."

"She takes care of you. She doesn't even see me."

"She feeds you," Johnnie says. He gestures at the shrimp salad. "You ought to eat that. Flies may get in it."

Anne picks at the shrimp salad. *La señora* sometimes makes a dish of fresh grilled fish and tomatoes and onions. Anne wishes she had asked for that instead. The shrimp salad tastes unpleasantly salty.

The hotel's ancient parrot perches on a tall brass stand on the other side of the patio. It shifts from foot to foot on its perch, rocking the stand slightly. The metal bottom of the stand makes a grinding sound against the tile of the patio. The floor there is worn and scarred, as though the parrot has been rocking for years.

The parrot's body is a dozen different colors, from peacock blue to teal to a rich sunset red on the wings. Its beak and claws are an identical pearly gray. It's an elegant bird. *La señora* claims that it is more than seventy years old.

"I think the doctor's screwing her," Johnnie says. He's still looking off into the kitchen after *la señora*. "I wonder where she is with that beer."

"The doctor?" Anne tries to picture *la señora* with the

skinny man in the porkpie hat and threadbare vest who comes to the hotel every day or so with his bag. He looks as starved as *la señora* is well fed, and his manner always seems near to panic. He stays close to the walls of the hotel, avoids the open patio. Anne suspects that he's practicing without a license, that it's discovery by the law that scares him.

"Do you think?" she says. "It seems unlikely. Him with her."

"Sure," Johnny says. "He doesn't want that air conditioner for *el señor*. *El señor*'s going to die no matter what. The doctor wants the air conditioner so he'll have a cool place where they can screw."

It's one of Johnnie's crazy ideas, and Anne is about to ask where he got it when *la señora* comes back with his beer. She has brought another rum-and-Pepsi as well. She sets the drinks before him as if she's making a special gift of them.

"*Gracias*," Johnnie says. He's pleased with himself for coming up with the word. He's flirting, Anne sees, and *la señora* ducks her head and bobs and can't seem to tear herself away from their table.

"You like to eat," *la señora* says to Johnnie. To Anne she says, "He likes to eat," as if Anne has only recently purchased him and still might not understand all his properties.

La señora produces an envelope with some postcards tucked in it, hands the cards to Johnnie. "The Alhambra," she says. "In Spain. Someone send them to us who stays here and then went there."

Johnnie leafs through the postcards, holding them up one by one for Anne to see before he lays them on the table. They show different views of a colorful fortress with a number of crenellated turrets. She looks at the rough stuccoed walls of the place around her.

Johnnie examines the back of one of the postcards. " 'The Moorish castle Alhambra required more than one hundred years to build,' " he reads. " 'Its walls, topped by thirteen towers, enclose grounds of more than thirty-five acres. Trees, flowers, and nightingale songs add to the scene.' "

"Lovely," Anne says.

"It is the truth," *la señora* says.

Johnnie picks another card, reads again. " 'The Alhambra was the last stronghold of the Moors in Europe. It was captured by the Christian forces of King Ferdinand and Queen Isabella in 1492.' Busy year for them."

"It is a busy year," *la señora* says.

"I'm pregnant," Anne says. She surprises herself with the statement. *La señora* raises her eyebrows, scrapes the pile of postcards back into their envelope, plucks the last one from Johnnie's hand. Anne is glad to see her go. She takes herself off to the kitchen and lingers just inside the doorway, not quite out of sight. Johnnie swivels in his chair to look at Anne, picks up the planter's hat from the table, puts it on.

"No," Anne says, lowering her voice, "not really. I just said that to get your attention. A joke."

"You've got my attention," he says. "You've always got my attention."

"I was sick this morning. Really sick, and I was afraid for a second I might be, but I'm not. It doesn't feel like that, otherwise. It must have been something I ate."

"The plantain chips last night at the cantina."

"That's what I thought. It must have been the damned plantain chips. They had a strange taste to them."

"Everything's got a strange taste here," Johnnie says. "We have the Lomotil if your bowels are in an uproar. They'll freeze your gut. Did you take them?"

"I took two," Anne says. "They're working fine."

"That's good, then," Johnnie says.

Across the patio, the parrot screeches, rattles the stand. It cries again, holding its bright wings out from its body as though it's drying them.

"We should teach it to talk," Anne says to Johnnie.

"Teach it to talk English," Johnnie says.

"You'd think someone would have taught it by now," Anne says. "All those years."

"Pretty Polly," Johnnie calls out to the parrot. "Cracker, cracker."

A man, an American, crosses the plaza toward them. He traverses the tail end of the procession, which is made up of people who are out with no apparent religious purpose at all, drunks and revelers. A few of them lack limbs or sport conspicuous scars, and they have medals pinned to their chests, as if they might be war heroes. They wobble down the road on metal crutches or clumsy prostheses. They are as drunk as the others, and they shout at the tall man as he pushes his way through them. He grins at Johnnie and Anne.

"Here comes Carl," Johnnie says. "Good old Carl."

Carl has broad shoulders, a large noble head, thick hair gone prematurely white. He comes to the hotel often to eat his lunch, and he's taken to sitting with Johnnie and Anne. He's from Wisconsin originally, though he lives in Granada now, runs the ice plant. He calls Johnnie and Anne his American friends. He and Johnnie often sit together in the afternoons and drink and talk. Anne thinks he is handsome and sad.

"He has a crush on you," Johnnie says.

"Like *la señora* has on you," Anne says.

"I'm serious. The guy has a fetish about you. I see that."

"He's sweet. Carl is a sweet man."

A dark boy of about twelve follows him across the plaza with a wheelbarrow. The wheelbarrow looks as though it's full of wet newspaper. Carl carries a clumsy bundle in his arms.

"He always asks questions about you," Johnnie says.

Anne hesitates just a second before she asks, "What questions?"

"What do you care?" Johnnie says. "Questions."

"What kind of questions?"

"Sweet questions."

Carl is on the patio now, and Anne motions for Johnnie to be quiet.

"For one," Johnnie says, and he's grinning, "your perfume. He wanted to know the name of the scent you wear."

Then he stands, says to Carl, "Hey, fellow." The boy maneuvers the wheelbarrow up from the plaza and stands looking at Carl, waiting for instructions. Water leaks from the wheelbarrow onto the patio tiles.

"Ice," Carl says.

La señora comes from the kitchen, wiping her hands on a towel. Carl goes to her and they chat for a couple of minutes in rapid Spanish. Anne has only her high school experience with the language, but she can follow a little. Carl is refusing money for something, for the ice. The ice is for *el señor*. There can be no payment, not for this ice. It is a gift.

Finally *la señora* stands to one side. Carl gestures at the boy, who peels the newspaper off the ice, takes a pair of cruel-looking ice tongs from the wheelbarrow, and plunges them into the sides of the shining block. His thin arms strain as he swings it out of the wheelbarrow and follows *la señora* into the kitchen. Anne hears her cursing him for dripping water on her clean floor. She calls him *el indio*.

Carl pulls a chair up to the table, puts down his package. He jerks his thumb back over his shoulder, toward the kitchen door. "*La señora*'s old man is dying. Stomach cancer—he's riddled with the stuff. The ice keeps him cool, helps him feel better."

"It's nice that you bring it," Anne says. The boy dashes out the kitchen door, skips down into the plaza, is gone. *La señora* stands in the doorway, glowering after him. She's got the ice tongs in her hand, then tosses them into the wheelbarrow.

"It's no problem," Carl says. "We mint the stuff. Hell, the Alhambra's one of our biggest customers."

"Ice for the broiling masses," Johnnie says. "That's really sweet."

"Sure," Carl says. "It's the only business to be in here." He waves an arm around the sunny patio. "You can get hot when you want, and when you want cool, you come to the ice plant. We made the ice you've got in your drink."

Anne's *limonada* has grown warm, and there are only a couple of slivers of ice left floating in it. Johnnie plucks a sizable shard of ice out of his drink and drops it into her glass. "There," he says, and smiles at her. "Cool."

"Ice, after all," Carl says, "what is there to it? It's just cold water."

"Very, very cold water," Johnnie says. He sounds quite solemn. Anne wonders how drunk he has gotten, sitting on the patio. She cannot remember how many drinks he has had this morning.

"But what a difference it makes," Carl says. "Ice." He seems entranced with the word.

"You'll have to take us on a tour of your plant," Anne says. The idea of a storehouse filled with great sweating blocks of ice appeals to her.

"Sure," Carl says. "Sure thing." He seems eager. "We're only operating at about half capacity now, but that's temporary," he says.

Johnnie taps the bundle that sits on the table. The brown paper is wrapped with string. "What've you got in the package, Carl," he says.

"Oh," Carl says. "Presents. I brought you folks some presents." He thumbs open a pocketknife with a wide blade, slices the strings, pulls open the paper.

"Uncle Carl," Johnnie says.

"Souvenirs," Carl says. He brings out a horrific carved mask, painted blue. The mask is made from half a coconut shell, polished smooth. It has a bulbous red wooden nose glued in its center. Carl hands the mask to Johnnie, who holds it against his face.

"Halloo," Johnnie says through the slit mouth. The planter's hat, which he has not removed, casts the shadow of its brim across the mask. Behind the eyeholes, the lenses of his sunglasses are utterly blank.

"Hush," Anne says to him. "Thank you," she says to Carl.

He brings something else out of the package. It's a small stuffed iguana. The long claws on its left front foot are bent back, and the leg is broken at the shoulder. Where the scaled skin is torn, a pinch of the stuffing leaks out, dry as sand.

"It got a little messed up," Carl says. "I'm sorry."

Anne doesn't say anything. Carl brings out a straw bottle holder. The word "Nicaragua" is woven into its side in bright thread. With his other hand he presents a pair of large leather sandals. He hands these things to Anne, then holds up his hand as if to forestall her thanks. She puts the sandals and the bottle holder into the large woven basket she uses as a purse.

"One thing more," he says.

He fishes in his shirt pocket for a second, a look of concentration on his face. He hands Anne a pair of earrings pinned to a small square of cardboard. They are little gold filigree shoes on fine chain.

"Oh," she says. "Oh my." They are attractive earrings. She holds them up in the light, slips the silver studs out of her ears, puts the new earrings on. They feel heavy, dangling from her earlobes.

"Perfect," Johnnie says. He has put the mask down. "These are some nice presents, Carl." He picks up the iguana and scoots it along the tabletop. It cannot stand with its broken leg, rocks over onto its back.

Anne doesn't like to see it lying there with its mouth open. It looks as though its tongue and palate have been varnished. She picks it up and puts it in the bag along with the other gifts.

"Nice damn presents," Johnnie says.

"Just a little something to say, you know, welcome to Nicaragua. Welcome to Granada." Carl is embarrassed by the praise.

"It's a nice way to say it," Johnnie says.

"Will you stop?" Anne says to him. He looks at her with an expression of mild surprise on his face. She can't stand it when he mocks people in this deadpan way. She can't stand him making fun of big lonely Carl, with his dramatic white hair.

"Listen," Carl says, and he leans forward across the table. "I wanted to talk to you. John? About what you said yesterday."

"What I said yesterday." Johnnie isn't committing to anything. He glances at Anne, to see if she plans to scold him for this latest response. She isn't looking at him. Instead, she's watching Carl, whose face seems to be betraying him.

His features won't stay still. They move like some awful thing is alive and restless inside them, or behind them. She hopes he won't burst into tears, and suddenly she wants to reach across the table and lay her hand over his.

"About the ice plant," Carl says. When Johnnie doesn't respond, he looks to Anne for help. She has none to give him.

"We could really use you," Carl says with a shrug.

"Use him?" Anne says. She turns to Johnnie, whose face is ashen. He shrinks back in his chair. He looks as though he'd like to pick up the mask and put it on again.

To Carl she says, "He told you he was going to stay in Granada."

"Sure," Carl says. "I've been thinking about taking on a partner for a while anyway, and then Johnnie here comes along. The timing is beautiful."

"I was drunk," Johnnie says. "We were all drinking." His voice is quiet.

"Did you sign something?" she asks Johnnie. "Did he sign anything?" she asks Carl.

"Tell the truth, we're pretty badly undercapitalized at this point," Carl says. "Underfinanced from the start." He's pleading, not with Johnnie now, but with her.

"You bastard," Anne says. She means it for Johnnie, but it is Carl who recoils. She rises from her chair. Johnnie is staring at her. She wishes she could see his eyes.

"With the right financing, though, the right guy, it's a sure thing," Carl says. His voice is shaking. He's got this whole speech rehearsed, and he's going to recite it from beginning to end, apparently, no matter what his audience does. "I mean, what's ice, just water, right? And water's free. We got the whole lake if we want it."

Anne stands above Johnnie, and she's got her glass gripped tightly in her right hand. She doesn't know what to do with it, so she sets it down on the table, hard enough that it collapses into itself with a tinkling sound. She turns and walks away from them, toward the now empty plaza.

Behind her, Carl is still talking. "It's a lock," he says. "No way to lose, to my way of thinking."

Johnnie says, "Annie, listen. Listen to me. Listen." He doesn't get up from his chair to come after her. As she walks, Anne notices a splash of blood on the front of her yellow sundress. She has gashed her palm on the broken glass. She closes her hand and the blood comes faster. She's walking through strewn flower petals and paper and discarded bottles.

"I'm bleeding to death," she says.

She goes on out into the plaza, blood spattering the paving stones in dime-sized spots. Her arm is streaked, her dress is a total loss. Johnnie talks to Carl in low tones. They don't know she's cut. "Think maybe you misunderstood me, Carl," Johnnie says. She winds her handkerchief around her hand.

She whirls, faces the patio. She's out near the bandstand now. "I'm bleeding to death, Johnnie," she says. She begins to be frightened by the amount of blood she's losing. The cut pulses, and it doesn't seem to be closing up.

The men come to the edge of the patio. "What are you doing out there?" Johnnie says. Then he sees the blood. "What the hell," he says. He comes to her, helps her to the bandstand. She sits on the end of the platform, rests her head against the wooden railing. "Just relax," Johnnie tells her. "Open your hand."

When she does, Johnnie whistles.

"That's a whopper," Carl says. While Johnnie wipes at her palm with the clotted handkerchief, Carl ducks into the hotel, then comes running back.

"Here," he says, and presses a small parcel into her hand. It is a chunk of *el señor*'s ice, wrapped in a cloth napkin. "Squeeze on this awhile."

Anne squeezes, gasping with the pain. Soon the ice numbs the cut. She is deeply grateful for the cold. In her grip, the ice begins to melt, mingles with the blood dripping from her hand, dilutes it. The napkin turns a light pink. Johnnie holds her hand above her head, and the pose makes her feel slightly ridiculous.

"We're going home," she says to Johnnie. To Carl she says, "No ice plant. Not for him."

Johnnie inspects the trickle of water running down her arm. It is slowly clearing.

"So," Carl says. "There's no deal, then."

"No," Johnnie says. "No deal."

When Johnnie flips the Cessna's master switch, nothing happens. No gauges, no lights, no engine. He sits stock still in the pilot's seat, closes his eyes, presses the switch again, off, on, off, on. Still nothing. His lips move. He is whispering to the plane, but whether he is cursing it or begging it, Anne cannot tell. She is barely able to breathe in the close heat of the small cabin.

She would not let *la señora* call the doctor about her hand, although Johnnie said that he thought she needed stitches. The old woman and Johnnie and Carl wrapped the cut themselves, taking turns with cotton batting and cloth strips and tape. The bandages and tape extend around her hand and wrist. One strip of tape goes nearly to her elbow.

Carl insisted on driving them to the airport. He owns an American car, its upholstery neat and whole but faded by years of unrelenting sun. The interior of the car carried the sugarcane smell of the local rum, and the smell of cigarettes clings to Anne's clothes. She holds the bulky basket full of his gifts on her lap with her good hand. She keeps the other hand against the lower part of her belly, refuses to look at it.

"Well," Johnnie says. His voice is thin and dry. He pops the door of the cockpit, hops onto the blacktop of the apron. "Looks like the battery went pretty far down. You hang on here," he says. "I'll go get somebody."

Anne decides not to go back into the terminal building to wait. It is a contemporary building, lavish, with slick marble floors and brightly painted plaster friezes on the walls. It's not as hot there, but she doesn't feel like walking.

In a few minutes, Carl's old Chevrolet Impala swings around the terminal building, edges through a gap in the security fence, and pulls up under the plane's left-side wing. Johnnie and Carl get out. It occurs to Anne that Carl must have been sitting in his car in the parking lot, waiting for them to take off, waiting to watch them leave.

Johnnie opens the Impala's hood while Carl fishes a pair of jumper cables out of the trunk of the car. One of the zeus locks on the engine cowling sticks, and Johnnie forces it loose with his screwdriver. He lifts the left side of the cowling to expose the battery, fastens the jumper cables to it. Carl clamps the cables onto the car's battery.

Then Johnnie tells Anne to crank the engine. "The key," he shouts. "Turn the key." Carl takes a couple of steps back from the plane, although he is already well out of the way. Anne switches on. The prop spoins, hesitates, spins again. The engine catches, and the whole plane vibrates with the roar of it.

Johnnie gives her the thumbs-up. She turns to look out through the blur of the prop.

Johnnie pulls the cables free of the battery. The wash from

141

the propeller riffles his hair, tugs at his clothes. He shuts the cowling, head averted to shield his eyes from the blast, and stumbles. For an instant Anne is sure that he will fall into the spinning propeller blades. Her heart rushes at the possibility. She starts up out of her seat, calls Johnnie's name.

Then the moment is past, and Johnnie coils the cables and tosses them onto the hood of the car. He waves a negligent hand at Carl, who leans against the Impala's driver-side door. Anne realizes that he expected Johnnie to be killed by the propeller too.

"Okay," Johnnie says as he climbs back into the pilot's seat, locks the door. "This time for real." As they taxi off the apron, Johnnie talks to the flight controllers in the Managua tower, who speak English. He wears a large black pair of headphones, so Anne only hears his half of the conversation. She wishes she could hear their voices, the strangely accented words, the assurance in the commands of these unseen men. Poised at the end of the runway, the plane is cleared for departure. Johnnie opens the throttle.

As they pass Carl standing on the apron, he raises his hand to them in a salute. The plane catches the air then, begins its long climb, and Anne doesn't want to move her bandaged hand to return the wave. Instead she nods at Carl, knowing even as she does that the gesture is too small to be seen.

The ground falls away under their landing gear, then the small rectangle of Carl's Chevrolet and the larger intersecting rectangles of the airport. Johnnie banks the little plane, brings it around to a northwesterly heading. Anne cranes her neck to watch the city of Managua slipping away behind them, its suburbs like a scattering of mushrooms. Beyond that, she can make out a gray haze lying on the land, and she imagines it to be Granada.

At the controls of the Cessna, Johnnie is completely efficient now, inspecting the flight instruments, checking his settings. He eases back on the throttle and brings the plane to cruising speed. He shows his pleasure in the plane through the softening of the lines of his angular face.

"You fly so well," she says to him. "If only you could always fly."

Johnnie barely acknowledges that she has spoken to him, and she wonders briefly if he heard her in the buzzing, rattling cabin. Then he reaches over and touches her on the shoulder. "What do you mean by that?" he says, and returns to his scan.

She means that she's glad the foreign earth has vanished from beneath her feet. She means that she trusts him to keep them suspended safely in the air, and to return them to that familiar country from which they started. Her anguished stomach is roiling again, though, and her hand pains her. "I don't know," she says.

Past the curve of Johnnie's skull, the stark treeless cone of a massive volcano fills the port window. It doesn't seem to change its position at all while she watches, despite their speed. A wisp of vapor hangs above its summit. Anne closes her eyes against the vision, and the plane shudders slightly as it passes through a thin deck of clouds and into the clear cold reaches of the upper air.

BOUNTY

It was a hot cloudless August day, and the sun heliographed off the windshield and side mirrors of Candles's truck as he drove past the county courthouse. He parked the truck at a slant against the curb, set the hand brake, and unfolded himself in a leisurely way out of the cab. He was a tall man who wore walked-over workboots bound up with duct tape, wore jeans that were too short for his long legs, the denim washed nearly white.

Three kids were lounging against a boarded-up storefront across the street, and they watched as Candles rummaged in the covered bed of the truck. He pulled out the slack body of a dog, slung it across his shoulders. He held its slim forelegs in his left hand, hind legs in his right.

The least of the kids finished the cigarette he was smoking and pitched the butt down a sewer grating at his feet. The three crossed the street, hands in their pockets, and took up position behind Candles. They gestured at the man and the dog, talking in quiet voices among themselves. The least one said, "What do you figure you'll do with that dog, mister?"

Candles ignored the question, kept his eyes on the sidewalk just in front of his feet. The boys conferred again, laughed. "You know it's dead, don't you?" the biggest one asked. The least one said, "Dummy," making sure his voice was loud enough to carry to Candles. They followed him as far as the courthouse doors and then abandoned him, went back across the street to their place.

Candles pushed through the swinging doors of the court-house. They shut behind him, and he paused a moment while his eyes adjusted to the relative dark of indoors. Then he proceeded down the hall and entered the first room he came to.

There was a pasty-faced character writing on some papers there who stopped the scratching motion of his pen when Candles entered. The character peered up at the dog settled across Candles's shoulders like a stole.

"This the sheriff's office?" Candles asked.

"Three doors down, on your left," the character said, and went back to sorting through his documents.

Candles went out, walked down the hall, counting doors. When he came to the third, he opened it. "Sheriff?" he said.

A woman inside said, "This is the sheriff's office." Candles stepped in, closing the door behind him with the heel of his boot. "Can I help you with something?" the woman said. She was small, seated behind a scarred wooden desk. She wore a blue uniform blouse that had a deputy's badge pinned to the flap of the pocket. There was a rack of rifles and shotguns behind her. The weapons were secured in their case with a brass padlock.

"I guess you can," Candles said to her. He lifted the dog off his shoulders and laid it on the tile floor. It was a medium-size brown dog that had been shot just at the base of its pointed skull. Its dark tongue lolled out of its mouth. "I believe you got a bounty on these," he said, and prodded the dog's corpse with his foot.

The deputy rose from her seat, circled her desk. She stood over the dog a moment. Then she called toward the half-open door of an inner office. "Sheriff Gallantin," she said. "Could you come here a minute?"

The sheriff came out of his office, a cup of coffee in his hand. He was a squat solid man with a belly on him; moved slowly. He wore metal taps on the soles of his shoes, and they rang against the uncarpeted floor of the office. He looked at Candles and then at the deputy, who directed his gaze to the dog. He grimaced when he saw it lying there.

"What is this?" he said. He gestured at Candles. "Did you bring that thing in here?"

"This man," the deputy said, and her voice was nicely controlled, "says that we're offering a bounty on dogs."

"Wild dogs," Candles said.

"The bounty is on coyotes, not dogs," the sheriff said. He set his coffee down on the deputy's desk. "You think we would pay people just to shoot their dog and bring it in?"

"This here's a coydog," Candles said. He knelt beside the animal, dug his hand into the ruff of hair on its neck, raised its head. The dog's loose jaw yawned open. "It's a cross between coyote and dog." He pointed the snout of the dog first toward the deputy, who stepped away, and then toward the sheriff. "Look there," he said, and gave the dog's narrow head a shake. "Don't that look like a coyote cross?"

"It looks like a dog to me," the sheriff said. He crouched

with a little difficulty next to Candles and grabbed at the dog's body, trying to get his arms under it as if he would load it back onto Candles's shoulders and that way be quit of it. When he couldn't get a good grip on the thing, he sat back. "You pick it up," he said to Candles. "Pick it up and get it out of here."

"Then you won't pay?" Candles asked. There was disbelief in his voice. "I got a whole truckload of these things parked out there," he said, and gestured behind him. "What am I suppose to do with those?" he said.

The sheriff stood, looked Candles over, appeared to consider. "It's not our office anyway," he said. He edged around Candles and the dog, stepped out into the hallway. "It's animal control you want. Let's get you down there to them and see what they have to tell you."

Candles watched him go. After a moment he grabbed the dog by its outstretched legs and hefted it back into its place. It weighed thirty or forty pounds, and he grunted as he rose from his crouch. "Thank you for your help," he said to the deputy. She smiled at him without saying anything, then returned to her desk. Candles left the office.

The sheriff was waiting for him up the hallway, at the door of the room Candles had entered earlier. Candles went to him, and the sheriff ushered him in. The pasty-faced character was still sitting there. "This is the man you want," the sheriff said, guiding Candles across the room. "This here's Leggy Gaines, your assistant dog warden."

"Animal control officer," Leggy said. He didn't stand. "What is it you want, Gallantin?"

The sheriff was grinning. "Where's Curtis?" he asked. To Candles he said, "Curtis is the real power around here. The head dogcatcher."

"Curtis is out on a call," Leggy said. "Somebody got a raccoon in their attic and it's tearing up the insulation. They're afraid it'll bite their kid or something."

"Well, I think you owe this man some money, Leggy," the sheriff said, indicating Candles. "He's gone and brought you a truckload of—" He paused. "What was it you brought?"

"Coydogs," Candles said. "I shot them. They been raiding my place, killing my sheep, so I set them up. They's more of them out there than what I killed. I imagine I'll get them after a while." He shifted the dog's body uncomfortably.

"Go ahead," the sheriff said. "Lay it on down. You found the place." He helped Candles set the dog on the floor. Leggy looked at it where it lay. "This man here'll give you your bounty," the sheriff said.

"I don't know," Leggy said. He had on a pair of little round glasses, and he slid them down to the end of his nose. "I recall your office has got that bounty on coyotes, but I don't believe we've set out any kind of a policy on feral dogs or whatever."

"Our office?" the sheriff said. "We don't pay any bounty. That's you."

"Somebody pays," Candles said. "I heard."

"We do pay a small bounty on rabid animals, which would apply to dogs," Leggy said. "We have to send their heads down to the lab in the capital to get tested before we disburse that money. Maybe that's what you're thinking of."

"What kind of a bounty did you hear about?" the sheriff asked Candles. "How much?"

"Five dollars a dog. And I got a truckful out by the curb."

"In that heat," the sheriff said, and wrinkled his nose.

"Did these animals exhibit any of the symptoms of rabies?" Leggy asked. When Candles didn't answer, he said, "Stiff-legged, staggering, snap at their shadow, walk into things like they're blind. Foaming at the mouth is what most people notice."

Candles studied the image a minute. "No sir," he said. "Not that I seen, they didn't."

"There you go, then," Leggy said. "It must be Gallantin's coyote bounty you're after."

"We got no bounty," the sheriff said.

"No more do we," Leggy said.

The three men stood in silence and regarded the dog in the middle of the floor. A fan that sat on a filing cabinet in the corner buzzed and rattled, sending a tepid stream of air from one side of the room to the other as it turned. Finally the sheriff said to Candles, "Well, let's see what we can do for you. You got anything in petty cash, Leggy?"

Leggy sighed, tapped a pencil against the bridge of his nose. "How many's he got?" he asked.

"How many you got?" the sheriff asked. "Six, seven?"

"Maybe fifteen." Candles said, "counting this one here."

"I don't think we can go five dollars on that many," the sheriff said. "How does two dollars a dog sound to you?"

"I don't know," Candles said. "Like I told you, I heard about a man that got five."

"Not around here he didn't," the sheriff said. "Two-fifty a head, and that's the most I ever heard of a man getting for a dead dog."

"Okay," Candles said. "If it's what you're offering, I guess I'll take you up." The sheriff looked at Leggy, who shrugged his agreement.

"You got it," the sheriff said. Candles started for the office door.

"Hold up," Leggy said. "You ain't leaving this mess here." He indicated the dog.

"Oh," Candles said, returning. "I thought you'd want it. For evidence or something."

"Well, I don't," Leggy said.

Candles bent and heaved the dog up. He balanced it across the back of his neck, and its legs hung down the front of his shirt. Its head trailed across his back, snout downward. The head bobbed loosely as Candles walked down the hall.

"Come on," the sheriff said to Leggy, who had not moved from where he sat.

Leggy said, "What is it you need me for?"

"To verify," the sheriff said. "We got to count the dogs he's got in his vehicle."

"You go," Leggy said. "You can count as good as I can."

"All right," the sheriff said. "We'll be back in a couple of minutes to give you the damage." He ducked out of the animal control office and followed Candles as he headed down the corridor.

Outside, Candles moved down the sidewalk with his stiff sweeping gait. Seeing what he carried, the couple of people that he met moved out of his way, rolling their eyes at the trailing sheriff as though they wondered when he was planning to haul in this demented larrikin.

One man took his eyes off Candles's figure and tugged at the sheriff's sleeve as he went by. "What you got there, Gallantin?" he asked. His breath was beery.

"Coydog," the sheriff said. He pulled himself free and continued on before the drunken party could form his next question.

The three kids who had followed Candles earlier stood gathered around the rear of his old mud-colored truck. When Candles reached it, he slid the dog off his shoulders and dropped it onto the sidewalk, where it sprawled. The kids stared at him, peered into the bed of the truck, looked back at Candles again.

Candles ignored them. He reached into the truck and hauled another dog out, holding it by the loose skin at its withers and its hindquarters. It was a fawn-colored dog of no particular breed, with heavy forequarters and a narrow back end, an almost hairless whip tail. He heaved it onto the sidewalk next to the first. It lay with its head bent under its body at an unnatural angle. He reached into the truck again, extracted a third dog, a brown lanky mixed-breed that had had its back broken by rifle shot, and deposited it with the others.

"Whoa there," the sheriff said when he caught up to Candles. "You don't want to do that." He caught the odor that boiled from the truck, and the low buzzing of flies. "This is no place to put them dogs."

"It's a pack of them," the least kid said. "I told you it was a bunch of dogs he had in there." The three stood looking at the short line of bodies on the sidewalk.

"Just coydogs," the sheriff said to them. "Wild dogs. Nothing to worry about."

"How do you plan to count them, then?" Candles asked. "We got to pull them out to count them." The bed of the truck was covered with a tarpaulin strung loosely over the high board sides. Candles leaned into the noisome space beneath the tarp, dragged another dog out, tossed it among the others.

"That'n there's a beagle," the least kid said.

Leggy came down the street in time to hear what the kid said. He was wearing a white uniform jacket. "I don't believe I'm going to pay for any beagle," he said. He pushed his way through the little group around Candles's truck. "You told me these were coydogs, not pets," he said to the sheriff. "That was your word for it." He turned to Candles. "And I might not pay for these others here either, until their authenticity is established," he said.

Candles loomed over him, and his eyes were dark. "You told me two-fifty a dog," he said. "You didn't say that about authenticity." He flexed his big hands.

"Well, where did the beagle come from, then?" Leggy wanted to know.

"How do I know where it come from," Candles said. "It was running with them others and I shot it."

"It's got trap marks," Leggy said. He bent down to the dog, which was a gray-muzzled beagle bitch. Its belly was swollen, lined with a double row of black teats. Leggy picked up its right forepaw, shook it. "I know trap sign when I see it," he said. "This leg's clear busted."

Candles's brow wrinkled. "Trap, shoot. I don't know. It was there with them others. They harry my sheep and drive them over a bluff or run them till they get a heart attack. They do it for fun," he said. He was breathing hard. "They don't even eat them."

The sheriff moved between them. "Why don't you just put them back in the truck," he said to Candles. He was hot and he spat his words. Candles stood where he was.

"They killed my cat too," Candles said.

"You pay that guy to kill dogs for you?" the least kid asked Leggy.

"Shoot, we could do that," the next biggest kid said.

"How much do you get per dog?" he asked Candles, who ignored him.

"And they got in my melon patch," Candles said. "Busted open them sugar melons like they was eggs."

"He won't never answer what you ask him," the least kid said to Leggy, hooking a thumb toward Candles. "There must be something the matter with him. I believe he's simple."

"Go ahead, ask him something," the next biggest kid said.

The biggest kid had perched himself on the tailgate of the truck. He peered into the darkness of the truckbed, counting silently to himself. In a minute he declared, "They's better'n ten, eleven dogs in there, what I can see. Pretty big dogs." He hopped down from the back of the truck. "Some of 'em been there a while, too," he said.

"Anyway," Leggy said to the sheriff, "reason I come out is because Curtis called. I told him what you all were up to and he said you better stand by, on account of he wants to get a look at what was brought in. He said he wouldn't authorize no bounty without his okay."

The sheriff leaned against the fender of the truck, stood up when he recalled the carrion in the bed. He sighed. "All right," he said. "We'll wait on Curtis. He say how long he would be?"

"He was wrapping up the raccoon situation when he called. He said it might be a while."

"You got any more pets in your truck?" the sheriff asked Candles.

"I got nobody's pets," Candles said. "Just wild dogs is all."

"Wouldn't surprise me none if they were somebody's," the least kid said. "It might be he just goes around grabbing dogs. I know a number of people that are missing their dogs around here." He looked at Candles with narrowed eyes.

"You want us to see?" the next biggest kid said. "Edgar'll go in there and check on if it's wild dogs or tame if you want." He pointed at the biggest kid.

"I'll do it for a dollar," Edgar said.

"No dollar," the sheriff said. "Don't you all have school?"

"It's summer," the least kid said.

"Okay then," the sheriff said. "You must have someplace you got to be. Why don't you take off?"

"Well, sure," the least kid said. He started to cross the street, and the other two went with him. "We just thought we might could help," he said. The three of them retired to their spot in the boarded doorway.

Once there, the least one got out the makings for a cigarette, rolled himself one, stuck it in the corner of his mouth, and lit it. The kids did scissors-paper-stone together. When Edgar, the biggest one, lost at that, he headed out for the store on the corner to get them all bottles of pop.

The sheriff said, "I think I'll go back to my office awhile. It's cooler there. You fellows come get me when Curtis shows up, won't you."

Candles looked worried. "I don't know about waiting," he said. "It's a long way to go, back to the mountain. I got to get back to my place."

"Stay or go. Whatever you want," the sheriff said. He started off down the street, got half the way to the courthouse before Leggy sang out, "Here he comes." He turned and, with the others, watched the white animal control van as it made its way along the street, coming toward them through the haze of pavement heat.

The brakes of the van whined as Curtis pulled to a stop beside Candles's truck. He stuck his head out of the driver's window, yelled, "This the place, Leg?" Leggy called back that yes, this was it. Curtis threw the van into reverse and backed into the spot next to the truck. When he cut the wheel at the last moment, the van thumped the truck, and its bumper dragged a little streak of primer from the truck's side.

"Damn," Curtis said, hopping out. He was a fat man with curly black hair, and he walked as though his feet pained him, taking mincing little steps. He bent down to inspect the scrape. "This your truck, buddy?" he asked Candles, who had stepped forward.

"It's mine," Candles said.

"I'm awful sorry," Curtis said. He pressed at the scarred paint with his fingers. "It don't look too bad, though," he said, standing up and dusting his hands against each other. "It ain't like you got a million-dollar finish on that thing in any case, is it?" he said, and laughed.

"No," Candles said.

"I always have trouble parking that wreck," Curtis said, jerking his thumb over his shoulder at the van. "We use to have an old panel truck, and I could just swing it around on a dime, but this new one." He shook his head. "You ask Leggy here, he'll tell you."

Leggy nodded his head vigorously. "Curtis can't park for anything," he said.

"What's this here?" Curtis asked when he saw the dogs on the sidewalk. He sniffed at the back of the truck, said, "It don't smell any better than it might, does it?"

"These dogs," Leggy said. "We talked about these on the phone."

"I thought you said coyotes. I had to come down and check out this truck full of dead coyotes for bounty, you said."

"I never said that about coyotes. Coydogs, is what he told me," Leggy said. "I never heard of them, but I figured you'd know."

Curtis turned to the sheriff. "I just snared a family of raccoons out of an attic of a house on the Tinder Road, and decided to check in before I went home. Nothing tire you out like fooling with raccoons. Just like little monkeys or something, the way they dash around."

From across the street, the least kid shouted, "That guy's been stealing dogs, Curtis. He's got Mrs. Shipley's little beagle dog right there in front of you if you look." He pinched his cigarette between his thumb and forefinger, dropped it on the sidewalk, ground it out with the toe of his tennis shoe.

"And somebody's German police dog too," the next biggest kid called out. "It's there in the truck. Edgar seen it. He told us."

Curtis snapped his head toward the kids, then back to the man. "There any truth in this?" he asked Candles, who said nothing, just backed up a couple of steps. "Sheriff?" Curtis said.

"I don't have any idea," the sheriff said. "He says he shot them running sheep on his place, and I'm as inclined to believe him as not. He's looking for a bounty price on them."

"Because we got some reports like that recently," Curtis said. "Folks missing their dogs. We thought might be it was a ring of thieves or something."

"I told him we'd give him two-fifty a dog," the sheriff said. "Your office and mine. But I guess we wouldn't have to pay him for the ones look like they were domesticated. Collars and such."

"It's more than that," Curtis said. "Statutes provide a stiff penalty if he's been killing pets. He could do time. I think you'd know about that, Sheriff Gallantin. As a peace officer and all."

Candles said, "Do time. For what?" He swept his arm over the dogs. "For this? Them's sheep killers. I lost twenty head, and just come into town because a fellow told me you'd pay." He looked a little panicked.

"I thought it was some funny business like that," Leggy said. "When he first come into the office. He give me a look up and down and it just about give me a chill."

"He said they were coydogs," the sheriff said. "I didn't know anything different."

"This beagle does look some familiar as I study it," Curtis said. He bent and prodded the dog with his forefinger. "I'll place it here after a while, if I think about it."

"You keep them," Candles said. He headed for the door of his truck, but Curtis was blocking the way. He veered aside, started to walk off down the street.

"He's getting away from you," the least kid said.

Candles picked up his pace when he heard the kid's voice. The sheriff trotted after Candles, then broke into a heavy run when he saw how fast the other man was moving. Still Candles pulled away, his long legs pumping under him. The two animal control officers stayed where they were.

"Whoa up, there," the sheriff called out as Candles neared the street corner. Edgar came out of the store then and blundered without looking into Candles's path. He had three cold bottles of pop in his hands, and his eyes widened as Candles collided with him. The impact sent the bottles spinning out into the street. Two of them shattered there, and the pop ran over the pavement and sizzled with carbonation. The third bottle spun on its side in the intersection.

Edgar and Candles sprawled together on the sidewalk.

When Candles got up to run again, Edgar clung to him, shouting. Candles tried to shake him off, grabbed the collar of Edgar's shirt in his wide hands. He tried to thrust the kid away from him, and Edgar's shoulder blades thumped against the sidewalk.

They were tangled that way when the sheriff came up on them. He drew them apart from each other and held on to Candles. "Don't you go anywhere," he said to Candles, who pulled away from him. He twisted the man's bony arm up behind his back and forced him to his knees. "Just cool down," he said into Candles's ear. Candles was trembling. Edgar continued to shout behind them.

"You fight with me and you'll wind up in a whole world of trouble," the sheriff said. He stood Candles up, pushed him against the brick wall of the store.

Edgar stood up and darted into the middle of the street. He kicked around among the shards of bottle glass, picked up the unbroken pop. He inspected it with a critical eye. "This's all that's left," he told the other two kids when they rushed up to him. They gathered around Candles and the sheriff, who was patting him down.

"Give him a good poke in the ribs," the least kid said.

"You ain't even got your nightstick, nor handcuffs," Edgar said. "He knocked me down and busted my pop. He like to killed me." He held out his scraped and bleeding hands as testimony.

"You ever heard of obstructing justice?" the sheriff asked them. When Candles stirred, the sheriff hissed at him, "You ever heard of resisting arrest?" Then, to the kids again, he said, "Scat."

They stood watching a moment longer. The least kid put his hands on his hips, pursing his lips like he intended to say something more. Then the three of them turned in a body and sauntered to the corner store. The storekeeper stood in his door, wiping his hands on his apron. "Everything all right, Sheriff Gallantin?" he said.

"Give them a soda, will you?" the sheriff said. The storekeeper led the kids inside.

Tucked into Candles's right boot, snug against his lean calf, the sheriff discovered a long bone-handled folding knife. He opened it, squinted along the blade, tested the edge against the hair on his arm. "Some sharp pig-sticker," he said.

"Skinning knife," Candles said into the wall.

The sheriff shoved him in the middle of his back, and his breath rushed out of him as he pressed against the brick. His lower lip began to bleed. "I'll ask you when I want to know something," the sheriff said. He closed the knife, slipped it into his pocket. He propelled Candles along the sidewalk in front of him.

"You busted him, Gallantin," Leggy said as Candles and the sheriff approached the truck and the animal control van. "We saw it. Plenty righteous," he said. The sheriff said nothing, kept Candles moving toward the truck.

"We got the evidence right here," Curtis said. He climbed out of the back of the truck wearing a white surgical mask over his nose and mouth. His hands were covered by a pair of thick leather gauntlets. He dumped the body of a young Alsatian onto the pavement and pulled the mask down around his neck.

"What are they doing with my dogs?" Candles asked. He spoke softly because of his injured lip. The sheriff threw open the driver's-side door of the truck. Candles craned his neck around to see what Curtis and Leggy were up to.

"Get in there," the sheriff said. Candles climbed into the

truck and sat staring forlornly out the open window at the sheriff, who closed the door.

"You got your keys?" the sheriff asked.

"Sure," Candles said. He dug in one of his pockets, held the truck keys up. They were secured by a couple of links of light chain to a round leather tag. Candles held the keys out as though the sheriff might want to take them from him.

"No," the sheriff said. "I don't want your keys. Just start this thing." He marched around the truck, said to Leggy and Curtis, "Get them dogs in the truck."

"Wait a second, Gallantin," Curtis said. "You got no jurisdiction here. You don't tell animal control what to do."

"No," the sheriff said. "I guess I don't." He leaned down and picked up one of the dogs. He grimaced at the hairy feel of its hide in his hands and sighed as he heaved its limber weight into the bed of the truck. It struck with a muffled thump against the other dogs.

He grabbed the forepaws of the Alsatian, but he couldn't lift the dog off the ground. After a moment's hesitation, Leggy took up the dog's back end, and they swung the heavy body over the board tailgate and into the truck. As the two of them loaded the rest of the dogs, Candles cranked the truck. The starter motor spun and finally the engine caught. Dark exhaust plumed from the tailpipe. Curtis stood back and watched.

The last dog to go into the truck was the beagle. When he had pitched it in, the sheriff walked back to the cab of the truck. "There you go," he said to Candles. "You're all loaded up. Now roll." He leaned into the window, speaking softly. "And don't come back here with another mess like this."

When Candles opened his mouth to speak, the sheriff held up a forestalling hand. "I don't need to hear it," he said. "I'm not sure exactly what went on here," he said, indicating the back of the truck, "and I don't believe I care to know."

"What do I do with them now?" Candles asked.

"Hell, I don't care," the sheriff said. "You got a shovel?"

"Sure," Candles said.

"Dig a big hole," the sheriff said. "Dump them in it. Cover them with caustic lime. Fill the hole back up."

"I never figured on nothing like this when I come down," Candles said.

"You bet you didn't," the sheriff said. He stepped away. Candles forced the truck into first gear, stalled it out. The truck rocked back to where it had been. Candles grimaced, twisted the key again, but the truck refused to start.

"Flooded it," Leggy said. Candles cranked the truck again, and this time it roared to life. He gave it the gas and bumped one wheel up over the curb as he pulled into the street, where he narrowly missed a sedan that was passing. The sedan's driver blew his horn, waved a fist. Candles turned the truck north and headed away from the men, out of town.

After he was gone, Curtis climbed into the animal control van without a word, slammed the door behind him, and pulled out of his parking space. "Curtis'll be okay here after a while," Leggy said. The van slowed for a stop sign, rolled through it, rounded a corner. "It's just he doesn't like people to order him around."

"Sure," the sheriff said. "Curtis is okay. I imagine I know how he feels." The two of them walked toward the courthouse together.

The three kids wheeled back onto the street, swigging their pop, at about the time Leggy and the sheriff reached the courthouse. As the kids were moving to take up their place at the storefront, a long-limbed redbone hound came wandering up the street and sniffed at the section of sidewalk where the bodies had lain.

"Check that out," the least kid said. "He don't even know it's a massacre of his own."

The redbone moved from one spot to another, snuffing. The least kid picked up a small stone from the street and shied it at the dog. The stone skittered off the pavement, and the redbone raised its head, pricked its ears. The other two kids pitched rocks as well. The redbone yelped, broke for cover. It holed up under an old Malibu wagon across the street and lay there, watching the kids warily from between the car's wheels.

"Hey," the sheriff called from the doorway. "You want to leave that hound alone."

"Okay," the least kid said. The three of them parleyed, then dropped the few stones they had gathered. Darting glances at Leggy and the sheriff, they disappeared down a dusty side alley.

Leggy spat dryly on the sidewalk and went on into the courthouse. The sheriff peered down the alley. He squinted after the kids, but the day was bright and the space between the buildings was filled with shadows. He shaded his eyes, couldn't make out their progress at all.

The redbone pulled itself out from under the Malibu, glanced around. When it saw that the kids were gone, it headed back up the street the way it had come. It zigzagged from one side of the road to the other, nose down, nails clicking against the hardtop.

The sheriff stayed where he was until the dog too was out of his sight. A big garbage bin stood next to him, just outside the courthouse doors. The sheriff patted at his pockets one after the other and at length withdrew Candles's skinning knife. He turned it in his hand, ran his thumb over its flawed bone handle. Then he tossed it into the bin, where it slipped down among the papers and crumpled pop cans and assorted trash to thump against the metal bottom. The sheriff pushed against the wide doors of the courthouse, which opened smoothly for him on their oiled hinges, and passed inside.

HORTON'S
APE

The baboon swayed back and forth, bandy legs bent, leathery hands resting on the straw at the bottom of its cage. It was gnawing a bone, and its jaws moved in perfect sync with its bobbing. It stared straight out at the guy who was taking its picture. The sun was bright in the backyard zoo at the Ponderosa Tavern, but the baboon didn't ever seem to blink.

Turley was drinking a beer and eating a hamburger at one of the little round tables out in the yard. His table sat at the base of the Ponderosa's giant saguaro cactus, about twenty feet from the ape and the guy with the camera. The guy was sweating in the sun. He kept backing up, trying to get all of the big ape in the viewfinder. Finally he crouched and snapped off a couple of shots.

He had one of those electronic cameras that spit the pictures out the front, and he pulled each photograph from it.

He kept looking from the pictures to the baboon where it stood in its cage. It wasn't moving anymore, just standing there and chewing. It beat a little tattoo on the floor of its cage with its knuckles.

After a minute the guy shook his head. "Jesus," he said. He held the pictures out toward Turley, flapped them at the ape.

"Pictures didn't come out?" Turley said. He was the only other person in the zoo, and it seemed like he ought to say something.

"It keeps moving," the guy said. The baboon spit the bone out. It was a knobby pale chicken bone. The baboon picked it up and added it to a low pile of bones at its feet. Then it reached out and shook one of the bars of its cage. It had a hand like a work glove, large and rough.

"What do you want a picture of that thing for anyway?" Turley asked. "It's got a face on it like a dog. I wouldn't want a reminder of it."

"For my kid," the guy said. He was a tall thin guy in a checked shirt. He pulled a handkerchief out of the back pocket of his jeans and ran it over his face. "I thought I'd like for my baby to see the monkey. We don't have anything like this around where I come from."

Turley leaned back in his chair and picked up his beer. "Why don't you get the little one a picture of something else?" he said. "There's lots of other stuff you could get."

He gestured around him with his glass. The yard was full of cages with animals in them. Right near Turley's table there was a tall wire-fronted cage full of brightly colored parrots. The parrots chattered and screeched and jumped from perch to perch inside. One of them climbed the mesh using its pearly claws and shiny beak. When it got to the top and couldn't go any farther, it turned upside down and levered itself to the bottom again.

Turley had been talking to the parrots when the guy came into the yard, clicking his tongue and saying, "Pretty bird, I'm a pretty bird." Only the one that climbed up and down knew how to talk back, apparently. It said, "Hello hello" from time to time.

"I think I'll keep on with the monkey a minute," the guy said.

Turley couldn't understand his dedication. There were a number of other animals that he liked better and that would outshine the ape in a picture. There was a high-shouldered mountain cat that was missing an eye in one cage, and a little brown bear in the neighboring cage. The bear kept trying to stick its nose into the cat's cage, but the cat wasn't paying any attention. A couple of glass cages had hand-lettered signs on them that said BOA CONSTRICTOR and PYTHON and ANA-CONDA, and those cages were full of coils and heaps of dark motionless snake.

Another cage had a sign on it that said GOANNA (FROM AUSTRALIA). The goanna was a four-foot-long lizard with blank lidless eyes and a tongue that flickered from its mouth in a gray blur. Other cages held a gila monster and an armadillo and a badger and a family of descented skunks and a tattered little red fox. In the shade of the back wall of the Ponderosa was a komodo dragon, which looked a great deal like the goanna. It was quite a little menagerie out behind the tavern, and Turley was pleased to have discovered it.

Inside the building was a fifty-gallon aquarium full of conger eels. The eels slipped through the spooky gray water and around one anothers' bodies in a way that Turley didn't like. They were a large part of the reason why Turley was eating his hamburger out back, even though it smelled like all those wild animals in the heat of the day.

"These things cost," the guy with the camera said. He tossed the two blurred pictures of the baboon down on Turley's table. Turley took them up and decided he wouldn't have known what they showed without having seen them taken. It might have been a woman in a fur coat, to the ignorant. "It costs about ten bucks for a pack of film," the guy said. "I figure that baboon owes me two dollars."

"You might get it from the management," Turley said. The guy was maneuvering up to the cage again with his camera. The ape began to bob.

"It's doing that deliberately," the guy said.

"Why don't you snap the pigs?" Turley said. A herd of six pigs had drifted across the yard half an hour earlier, first heading in one direction, then the other. They were rangy narrow pigs with sharp hooves and dark hairy faces. They were handsome animals, and Turley had tossed them the pickle wedge from his lunch on their second pass through. The lead boar snuffed it and passed it up, and the other pigs simply trotted over the pickle where it lay in the dirt. Turley didn't know if the pigs were connected with the zoo behind the Ponderosa or not. It seemed to him that they might just be out foraging.

"What pigs?" the guy asked. He had his camera up to his face, still looking for a shot.

"They were here awhile ago," Turley said. "I imagine they'll be back if you wait on them."

The baboon had stopped its bobbing, retreated to the back of the cage. It stood there with its long hairy arms wrapped around its head. The pelt was thin at the armpits, and its skin there was pink.

"That's a good pose," the guy said, and he went right up to the bars to get his shot. He pressed the shutter button and the camera whirred and a piece of film slid out of the slot. The baboon drew its lips back from its teeth and made a long low hissing sound. It kept its arms over its head. "Oh yes," the guy said.

"I think I wouldn't do that," Turley said. The baboon blinked and the guy took another picture. As he straightened up, the ape darted to the front of the cage and shot one arm through the bars. It grabbed the guy's wrist and pulled his arm into the cage with it. The guy tried to pull away and the baboon drew him back in, slammed him against the bars.

"Hey," the guy said. "Jesus." The baboon had some terrific strength, and it handled the guy with no problem at all. He slapped at it with his free left hand, and it snagged that one too. The guy stood there with both his hands inside the cage and his chest against the bars. The baboon hooted. The guy was shouting into its face. "Let me go," he said. His voice was high with fear.

Turley stood and went over to them. The guy was still shouting, cursing at the baboon. Turley figured the ape could break the guy's arms if it wanted to, but presently it was just holding him there. Whenever he pulled away, the ape took a firmer grip and pulled him back toward the bars.

"Give it the camera," Turley said. He didn't want to get too close. All the animals around them were upset with the guy's yelling. The mountain cat paced around in its cage, snarling. The bear rolled over and over in its straw. A little woodpecker flew out of its hole at the very top of the giant cactus.

The guy didn't appear to hear Turley. "Get me loose," he screamed. "Make it let go!"

"I bet it wants the camera," Turley said. He said it slowly, so the guy would get the idea and stop panicking. The baboon's strong fingers were really digging into the guy's flesh, and he sounded like he was in some pain.

Turley had carried his beer over with him, and he tossed it on the baboon. "Scat," he said. "Get back there." The beer caught the baboon in the face. It blinked and grunted and looked at Turley, but it didn't loosen its grip any. The beer dripped down its long snout and beaded in its coarse hair. The baboon shook its head, and its thick tongue crept out of its mouth. It licked at the droplets of beer.

The guy was crying now. Turley decided to take a chance. He reached into the cage and pulled the camera out of the guy's grip. The guy's hand was white and hooked into a claw. Turley flipped the camera back into a corner of the cage. The baboon turned its head and watched it go. It landed on the straw with a sharp crack, and the baboon scampered after. It picked the camera up and turned it over and over in its clever hands, peered into the lens. It pulled a developing photograph out of the slot with its teeth.

The guy fell back on the ground and crawled away from the cage. Turley stepped away too. "My God," the guy kept saying. He was sitting up and rubbing at his forearms. His shirt was torn there and under the sleeves. The seams had let go when he tried to pull out of the baboon's grip.

"That was something," Turley said. "That's some strong ape." He went back to his table and sat down, took a bite of his hamburger. The guy stood up and worked his fists, flexed his arms. It looked like nothing was broken.

In the cage, the ape triggered the camera, and another picture slid out and fluttered to the floor of the cage. "It's got my camera," the guy said. He was breathing hard, and his face was red. Turley just looked at him. The guy stood there with his hands on his hips for a minute; then he went into the Ponderosa, and the wooden door slammed shut behind him.

Turley took the last bite of his hamburger and regretted the loss of his beer. He decided against getting another one. He was headed back home, and he had a couple hundred more miles to go if he wanted to get out of the state before he stopped for the night.

He watched the ape. It had used up all the film in the camera, and the pictures lay around it. It wasn't paying any attention to the pictures, and Turley wondered what they looked like.

The baboon sat motionless on top of the camera, staring out the front of the steel cage again. It was a gray-furred ape with short legs and broad shoulders and a long low head. Its rear end was naked and pink, and it made Turley uncomfortable to look at it. The ape had ears a lot like a man's. Its long arms hung down at its sides. Its feet were just about the same size and shape as its hands. It sat there and hooted softly to itself.

"Got a prize, didn't you," Turley said to it. It turned to look at him and then went back to its meditation. Its long fingers twitched.

The door to the Ponderosa opened and the guy who had lost his camera came back into the yard. A short bald-headed fellow came after him. He was the guy who had taken Turley's order and brought him his food, and Turley figured he probably owned the place. A plastic tag pinned to his shirt said "Horton."

Horton was carrying a push broom with him, and he had a length of green garden hose looped over his shoulder. The guy said something to Horton, but the parrots near Turley had started up their noise again—they had gone quiet when the ape grabbed the guy—and Turley missed what he said. The guy looked agitated.

Horton dropped the hose and went to the baboon's cage. He stood gazing in, and Turley couldn't read the expression on his face. He looked to be about sixty years old, and he had thin lips and a crooked nose. His right eye was nearly swollen shut with some kind of an infection. Turley figured he had a dose of pinkeye.

Horton slipped the push broom through the bars of the cage and waved it at the baboon. When the ape didn't move, he shoved at it with the head of the broom, and it spilled backward off the camera. Horton tried to hook the camera with the broom, but the ape was there ahead of him, picked it up and cradled it and scuttled into a corner of the cage. When Horton circled to get near it, it ran to the other side of the cage. As it moved over toward him, the guy in the checked shirt backed up a couple of steps.

Turley went to where Horton stood. "I thought that it might take that broom away from you," he said.

Horton looked at him for a second, and the expression on his face didn't change at all. His swollen eye made it hard to tell what his mood was. "Yah," he said. "The ape knows not to fuck with me." He turned to the ape. "You're costing me money," he said. "You're making me trouble." The ape held the camera to its body with its left arm, like a runner holds a football.

"It really wants that camera," Turley said.

Horton turned back to him. "Did you give the ape this man's camera?" he said to Turley. He gestured at the guy in the checked shirt. The guy gave Turley an angry look.

"It was pulling his arms," Turley said. "It had hold of him and wouldn't let go. You ask him."

"I ast him," Horton said. "He said you gave his camera to it."

"You wanted my help," Turley said to the guy. "It seemed like the thing that would make it let go."

"It would of let go without the camera," the guy said. "It used up all my film. Look at that."

Horton used the broom to slide the pictures out of the cage. Some straw and manure and a couple of chicken bones came with them. The baboon didn't seem interested in the pictures. It stayed crouched where it was. Horton gathered the pictures into a stack and handed them to the guy, who leafed through them.

"What are these?" the guy said. "There's nothing on them."

"What did you expect?" Horton said. "The ape took them."

"You owe me for the film," the guy said. Horton said nothing. He put down his broom and hooked the garden hose up to a spigot on the back wall of the tavern near the komodo dragon.

The guy put the pictures down on a table, and Turley picked them up and leafed through them. Mainly they were close-ups of the ape, dark pictures full of fur and teeth and blurred nostrils. Some of them were chewed and bent and damp. There was one tilted photo of the bars of the cage and the Ponderosa and the cage of colorful parrots. Turley thought he saw the top of his head in a corner of the picture.

"I'll give you a buck for this one," he said.

The guy snorted at him. "What would you want it for?" he said.

Horton came toward them, dragging the hose. He had turned the water on, and the joint at the spigot was hissing and fizzing. "Sell it to him," he said. "Curiosity item."

"It's a picture with me in it," Turley said. The guy took the picture from him and looked at it. He shook his head and handed it back to Turley.

"You can have it," he said. "But how it's a picture of you I don't know. It just looks like a jumble to me." Turley tucked the picture into his pocket.

Horton pointed the nozzle of the hose at the baboon. "I'll open up and spray it off the camera, see," he said. "Soon as it moves, you grab your camera up out of there and you're okay."

"No," the guy said.

"You do it, then," Horton said to Turley. "You're the one that give it the camera, after all."

"Okay," Turley said. "Just make sure you get it away before I get in there with it." He didn't want to put his hand in where the ape could pop his fingers if it took the notion.

"I'll take care of the ape," Horton said. "You take care of the camera." He turned the nozzle and got a good steady stream of water. When he played the spray over the baboon, it shrieked like a woman. The mammals and birds in the cages all around shrank back from the noise. The reptiles took no notice at all.

The baboon stood up off the camera and leaped and swung by one arm from a bar in the ceiling of the cage. Horton kept the water on it and it swung arm over arm to the other side of the cage. On the last swing it missed its grip and fell to the bottom. It sat there with its back to the men, and Horton kept on spraying it. The water made a drumming sound against the ape's hide. The inside of the cage was slick and dripping.

Turley reached into the cage and picked up the camera. A little water from the hose splashed him, and it was cold. The camera's case was wet, and some water dripped out of the picture slot when he handed it to the guy. Horton turned off the water and they all backed away from the cage to see what the ape would do. It just kept on sitting there, and Turley wondered if the fall had hurt it or something. Horton coiled up his hose.

The guy was checking out his camera. He punched the shutter button and the camera hummed, but no picture came out. He opened it to make sure it was out of film. "How do I know if it still works?" he said. He shook the camera to get all the water out of it.

"Let it dry up," Turley said. "It'll be okay."

Horton unhooked the hose from the spigot. He got his broom from where he had laid it and went back into the Ponderosa. The guy started after him. "Hello," the one talking parrot said as he passed its cage.

"Now you got a story to tell your baby," Turley said.

"I didn't want a story," the guy said. "I wanted a picture." He headed on into the place.

Turley looked at the ape. It was small with its fur plastered against its skin. It had great long arms, but it was the size of a child otherwise. It had its arms wrapped over its head again and it was swaying back and forth, from foot to foot. Its naked butt was a shocking color against its soaked fur.

"Hey," Turley said to its back. "That guy's gone now." It kept on, lifting one foot after the other, grunting.

Turley circled the cage so he could check on the ape. When he got around to it, it turned from him and sat looking the other way. Turley laughed. He went around the cage again, and the ape turned again. It wouldn't face him. He went to

175

the table where the guy had left his pictures and picked them up. He was leafing through them when Horton came back into the yard.

"What do you want to look at those for?" Horton said. "You got the thing itself right there in front of you."

Turley put the pictures down. "It won't look at me," he said. "I think it got its feelings hurt."

"You bitch," Horton said to the ape.

"It's not so bad," Turley said. "It was just curious and the guy got a little close with his camera, is what happened."

"That's all the more you know," Horton said. "That guy was lucky he didn't pull just a stump back when he tangled with this ape here." He looked at the baboon. "Bastard," he said.

"It bites, huh?" Turley said.

"Sure," Horton said. "Look at the choppers on that thing. It's got a jawful of teeth like a goddamn Rottweiler. Bite through your bone, no sweat."

"I'm glad it didn't get its hooks into me, then," Turley said.

"You cost me money every time I turn my back," Horton said to the ape. "I ought to just put a bullet into you and let you die."

"It's done this kind of a thing before?" Turley said. "Took a camera or whatever from a person and wouldn't let it go? You looked like you knew what to do with that water hose."

"Sure it's done it before," Horton said. "It'll take a woman's pocketbook or a kid's toy or the hat off a man's head. It's a regular magpie. It took the walkie-talkie off a state trooper one time not too long ago. He was in here to get a sandwich and he wanted to look at the ape. He'd heard about it and he hadn't seen anything like that up close before."

"Not many folks have," Turley said. "It's one of the chief appeals of the place, I expect."

"I thought for sure we were going to have to kill it that time," Horton said. His voice was rising as he spoke, and his swollen eye watered. The eye looked painful to Turley, and Horton seemed like he was getting some infection in the other one as well. Turley wished he wouldn't get so excited.

"The trooper felt ready to do it," Horton said. "He wanted to go get the riot gun out of the squad car and let the baboon have it. I think it was the noise that the radio made—that was the attraction."

"Sounds like a tricky situation," Turley said.

"It was. I told him that it was just a joke the ape pulled and that it never even knew what it was stealing. I got it from a guy that had a little traveling circus. It was part of the ape's act that it would dash into the crowd and snatch an item from somebody and run off, climb the center pole to the ceiling of the tent. The person always got back the umbrella or whatever it was at the end of the show."

"It was trained to do what it did," Turley said.

"Sure it was," Horton said. "It could do other things too. It could ride a little scooter that they had for it in the center ring. It could play 'America' on a series of horns. They decked it out in a spangled vest and a cowboy hat they stuck on its head with adhesive. I got the different costumes the circus guy had for it. They're inside behind the counter. I used to dress it up, but I don't anymore." Horton pulled out a chair from one of the tables and sat down facing the cage. "I thought I could make some money off of the thing, but it's just costing me," he said. "It'll cost me this place after a while."

Turley looked at Horton with his swollen eyes and his ratty bar and all his animals that screeched and ate and his ape that was embarked on a ruinous course. He was tempted to take the ape off Horton's hands. He figured they could lash the ape's cage into the back of his truck and he could get it home.

He imagined a way to leash the ape and string a wire so that it could run across the yard and leap and play and even climb the tired little dogwood that grew there. He had seen an arrangement like that for big dogs, and he knew he could work it out to his satisfaction and the ape's. It seemed like a better idea the more he thought about it. He lived alone, and there was no one to tell him that he couldn't undertake it.

"What does it eat?" he asked Horton.

Horton just sat there a minute before answering. Finally he said, "Eat? It eats everything. That's a part of the problem right there. It ate a couple of buzzards one time."

"Buzzards," Turley said. He had never heard of anything eating buzzards before, not even other buzzards.

"Sure," Horton said. "Some kids that were back here one time let it loose out of its cage. I had a couple of big African vultures in a cage across the way, and the kids just watched the thing as it went and opened the vulture house and got in there with them and pulled the birds apart and ate them. The kids were bug-eyed. That's why we don't let kids into the zoo anymore without their parent or guardian."

"I'm surprised you let anyone back here after that," Turley said.

"I came out here to see what all the squabbling was, and here's this ring of kids and there was the ape sitting in the wrong cage with a vulture wing in either hand. It was covered in feathers and blood and it had the head of one of the vultures stuck in its mouth. I didn't know what I was looking at."

"Some kind of a devil," Turley said.

"It was crouched down on its haunches and flapping those wings up and down, up and down, like it wanted to fly. The wings were busted in any number of places and they made an awful creaking noise when the ape waved them."

"I never heard of anything like it," Turley said.

"No," Horton said. "The ape's got an evil inclination. It got a stick from somewhere and reached across a space and poked the eye out of the mountain lion. I couldn't tell you where the stick came from. That's why I've got its cage way in the middle, out from the others."

"And even with all your caution it makes so much trouble," Turley said. He didn't so much pity the baboon anymore as admire it. He looked at it again and tried to imagine it in a little spangled suit pushing a scooter around in a circle, or tooting at a row of horns. It was a hard picture to get in his head. The ape scratched at itself like it was picking a scab.

"They say these baboons live in great gangs in Arabia. They live in crevices in the cliffs," Horton said. "The circus guy told me sometimes hundreds of baboons will pour out of a gorge and run down a bunch of elands or kudus or some other herd animal. He said the noise they make when they have killed is deafening. He said when you lie in your tent at night and listen to them scream, the sound is nearly human."

"Does this one scream like that?" Turley said.

"It screams, but it just sounds like an animal to me. Maybe it's different when you get a bunch of them together, but I hope I never find out." Horton got up and walked over to the cage and made a clucking noise at the baboon. It looked at him but didn't move.

"I never even named it," Horton said. "They called it Bobo or JonJon or some stupid thing when it was in the circus, but I didn't even bother to learn exactly what. The ape snarled and shouted for two entire days when I put it in the cage back here. I guess maybe it knew what pass we would come to in time." He got up, started off toward the Ponderosa.

"What pass is that?" Turley asked him.

"The guy with the camera," Horton said. "I had to promise him I'd kill the baboon so he wouldn't sue me."

"You don't have to listen to him," Turley said. "He won't know anything about it. He doesn't live around here. He said he didn't."

"He might come back," Horton said. He went inside.

It was hot out in the yard, and Turley felt strange, alone there with the animals looking at him. He gathered up his plate and his glass off the table, his fork and his knife.

"I guess you've had it," he said to the baboon.

It clapped its hands together and hooted at him. It held its hands up palm out, made fists, opened them, curled its hands again. On the other side of the yard the six pigs came out of the scrub, noses down, rooting. One small sow made her way past the snake cages and came to the pickle Turley had thrown out there. She dropped to her front knees and began to munch it.

The ape continued to gesture at Turley. It flapped its hands on its loose wrists and wagged its head.

"I don't have any more food," Turley said. He wondered how long it would take Horton to get a gun, or whether he was planning to do it with poison or something. He walked to the cage. "What do you want?" he said. "Do you want the plate? Do you want the utensils?"

The ape stood and walked to the door set into the side of the cage. It grabbed the bars with both hands and stood swaying. It peeled its lips back from its gums, and Turley saw its big teeth, great large yellow teeth. It grunted and sneezed, snapped at a fly that buzzed past its head.

Turley handed his plate in through the bars, and the baboon took it and held it up before its face. It licked the plate. Turley held out the knife and fork, and the baboon reached out for them. It took them from his hand without touching him at all. It didn't look at him. The thick hair on its head was swept back in a kind of a duck's-ass hairdo. Its ears stuck out from the sides of its head.

"Okay," Turley said. He bent down to look at the fastening on the door of the cage. It was a complex braid made out of leather, a series of knots and twists in a thick piece of rawhide. Turley figured it had to be like that to keep the ape from working it loose. The ape had hands like a thief. Turley picked at the rawhide for a second, and the ape hooted.

Turley flicked out the big blade on his pocketknife, started to saw on the fastening. "I'm going to open the door for you," Turley said. "That's all I'm going to do. After that it's up to you." He cut through the leather and pulled the thong out of the door, and the door swung open.

The ape stood on the threshold for a moment, looked around it, behind it, to the left and right, as if it expected a joke. Then it looked at Turley and drew its lips back from its teeth. It hissed and leaped out the door, and Turley backed up, swearing. The ape hit him in the middle of his chest going full speed and wrapped its long arms around him and the two of them fell to the ground.

The ape was damp and smelled of meat and musk. It squeezed and Turley felt as if his ribs would give. He put his hands on either side of the ape's head and shoved, trying to drive it back from him. The ape opened its mouth, turned its head, and bit down on Turley's thumb. Turley screamed, and the ape screamed too, and they lay there together in the dirt of the yard and shrieked at each other.

The ape leaped up and hit the ground running. Turley

took a breath gingerly. He didn't know if anything was busted inside him, and he didn't want to worsen the situation. His thumb ached like a bastard and he refused to look at it. It was still attached to his hand and that was all he cared to know about it. He rolled over onto his stomach and yelled after the ape. There were no words to what he was yelling. It was just noise, and the ape paid no attention to him at all.

The pigs had taken off running when the ape first came out of the cage, and they were fast, but the ape was faster. It streaked across the ground, bending low. Most of the pigs were at the edge of the yard, almost among the scrub, but the one that had stopped to chew on the pickle was well behind the others. It still had the pickle in its mouth and it was squealing and racing hard when the ape caught it up by one back leg. It dropped the pickle.

The ape didn't miss a beat in its stride. It dragged the young pig by the leg, grunted, and leaped onto the lowest limb of the great saguaro cactus in the center of the yard. The pig dangled, yelped, bounced off the limb. The ape began to climb.

It went up the cactus quickly, stopping from time to time to disentangle the thrashing pig from a clump of thorns on which it had caught fast. The ape's naked rump showed up vivid pink against the green mass of the cactus. The sun was directly over the yard, in Turley's eyes as he stood looking up, and the ape's butt was the easiest thing for Turley to see. He watched the ape's progress as it toiled there above the ground. It went twenty feet up, thirty, and it didn't seem to feel the cactus needles at all.

The baboon sat on a thick limb about three quarters of the way up the saguaro. It gripped the branch with its feet, holding the pig in its strong hands like a slice of watermelon.

It was gnawing on the pig and bouncing gently, rocking the branch. It appeared to think that it was a part of some other place and some other time. The ape had forgotten that it had spent its life in a circus riding on a scooter and sitting in a cage out back of the Ponderosa Tavern. It thought it had spent its whole life high in some ancient pipe-organ cactus, chewing on an animal. Turley wondered if it tasted kudus when it bit the pig.

"What in hell's this?" Horton said. Turley hadn't heard him come back into the yard. He had a Remington twelve-gauge pump shotgun cradled in his arms. He looked at Turley. "You crazy bastard," he said, and he poked at Turley with the muzzle of the gun. The pig was still screaming high above them. Turley thought for a minute that Horton was going to shoot him.

"You let it go, didn't you?" Horton said. "What did you want to do a thing like that for?" A light red rain pattered down the trunk of the cactus.

Horton threw the shotgun to his shoulder and fired. He jerked the trigger, and the shot tore into the cactus half a dozen feet below the ape. A milky spray flew. He worked the slide of the gun and fired again, got a little closer this time. The ape screamed and climbed a couple yards higher, where there were no more limbs. It clung to the trunk of the cactus and yelled and shook the body of the pig at them. Horton fired a third shot, and this time Turley couldn't tell where the load went.

"Do you shoot?" Horton said to Turley.

"I don't want to shoot it," Turley said. "It's your ape."

"You shoot it," Turley said. He thrust the shotgun into Turley's hands, and when Turley took it the metal of the barrel was hot. The smell of burned powder was heavy on the gun. "The doctor tells me I got conjunctivitis," Horton said. "When I look up there I see two apes."

Turley stepped closer to the cactus, sighted along the raised barrel of the Remington. His bitten thumb throbbed. He centered on the baboon, fired. The gun kicked back against him and the ape vanished out of his sight. He didn't know whether he had hit it or not. Something crashed down along the cactus trunk toward him, took a bounce, spun in the air, landed at his feet. It was the pig, and he was spattered with its blood. Its body was in a terrible state. Turley lowered the shotgun.

"Did I get it?" he said.

Horton was squinting up at the cactus. "You got the pig," he said. "The ape's still there."

Turley's eyes were smarting from looking into the sun, and it took him a minute to spot the ape. It was at the top of the cactus, holding on with one hand, its feet, and its thick tail. It was leaning in a drunken way, and Turley thought that he might have hit it after all. He watched it to see if it would fall without his having to do anything more. He was breathing hard. The ape stayed where it was.

"Shoot it," Horton said. Turley raised the gun again, and the ape watched him do it. He pulled the trigger, and the top of the cactus blew away. The ape fell. It fell into branch after branch and caromed off, throwing out its hands, grabbing, stripping away needles and cactus flowers. At the last it caught and clung to a branch above the men and swung there. Turley thought for a second it might pull itself up again, and he half wished that it would. Then it closed its eyes and let go.

Horton shouted to warn Turley, but Turley was fascinated watching the beast fall through the air and did not move out of the way. The body of the ape landed on him and knocked him to the ground. The gun flew out of his hands, and Horton had to duck it to avoid getting hit. Turley lay there under the ape. He tried to push the thing off of him, but his right arm wouldn't do what he wanted it to.

Horton crouched over him, heaved the ape away. It rolled loosely in the dirt, and its arms tangled under it.

"Are you okay?" Horton said.

"No," Turley said. "I think it busted my collarbone." He had broken his collarbone in a football game in high school, and it had felt just like this, hot and oily and swollen under the skin of his shoulder. He laughed, and it hurt him to do it, but he kept on.

"It fell right on you," Horton said, and it looked like he wanted to laugh too. "You just stood there like you planned to catch it or something."

He helped Turley up, and Turley gasped at the pain in his shoulder and it dried up his laughter. They stepped over the sprawled body of the ape without looking at it. The parrots in their cage started squawking again. "Hello hello," the one parrot said. The two men went on into the tavern, and they left the shotgun and the pig and the ape behind them, lying in the small shade at the base of the cactus.

ODOM

Odom squats beside the fresh-cut stump of a hickory tree. The heavy gnarled trunk of the hickory lies in cubit sections, ready for splitting, at the edge of the small clearing. Odom clasps a slender length of slow-burning fuse in his left hand, marries it to the wooden kitchen match he holds in his right.

The fuse runs to two sticks of dynamite, unpacked now from their thick waxy skins, capped, and tamped into a hollow under the hickory stump. Odom peers at the flame, shields it with the bulk of his body from a light breeze that has sprung up. Still the flame dies.

Odom tosses the spent match away, and his son hands him a fresh one, which he strikes against the dry leather upper of his boot. The son kneels, breathless, presses his solid shoulder against his father's, cups his hands around the burning match. The fuse smolders, fires, and Odom drops it. He and his son scramble away crabwise, clamber over a windfallen oak, and drop prone in a drift of leaves, not daring to look past the defilade at the charge they've planted. A minute or so passes.

"It's gone out," the son says.

"I don't believe so," Odom says, head down among the stinking windrowed leaves. "I got it lit pretty good."

Before he finishes the sentence, the explosive detonates. Odom hears only a dull thud, winces at the painful pressure inside his ears and against his eyeballs. He feels suddenly heavy where he lies, thickened, and his belly presses into the cool ground. The leaves whip and rattle around his head. Dust patters down on him, powders his shoulders and hair, the back of his neck. He can taste it on his lips.

Beyond the windfall, the stump rises, turning, into the air. A slab of wood as thick as a man's arm whickers by overhead. At Odom's elbow, a distressed copperhead slides out from under its blanket of leaves and cobwebs and slips away, tongue flickering from between its delicate triangular jaws.

When Odom opens his eyes, he sees that his son is pointing over the windfall and laughing, but he can't hear the sound. A drifting pall of smoke gets into his eyes and his throat, makes him cough. "What," he says. "What is it?" His own voice makes a dull, distant sound in his ears, like a dog's barking somewhere. He looks where his son points, in front of them and above their heads.

At first there seems to be nothing extraordinary there, just the knobby greenless branches of a tall black locust tree and behind those the bright bland horizon-line of the next ridge over and the vanishing copper disk of the sun. Odom decides that he must be looking in the wrong place. Then he spots the hickory stump, blackened twisted roots to the sky, caught a dozen yards off the ground in the limbs of the locust.

"Too big a blast," Odom's son says, the words sounding flat and pinched as though they come to Odom through a piece of iron pipe.

"I thought I was deaf there a minute," Odom says. He is still crouched and tense, but his son is up and out of their place already. "Till I heard you talk," Odom says. The son is at the crater that the explosion made, tipping clods of dirt back into the ragged hole with the side of his foot, still looking up at the suspended stump. It is trapped in the crotch of two principal boughs. Odom waits another moment to see if it will fall.

When it doesn't, he rises to his feet, grimacing at the popping of his hinges and bones, and joins his son at the hole. The smells of cordite and nitroglycerine and singed wood are strong around them.

"Did you see it go?" he asks.

"No," the son says.

"Me neither," he says. "I was just staring into the ground."

"It must of went up like a mortar," the son says. He tucks the branch saw into his belt and levers himself onto the lowest limb of the locust tree, at the height of his chest. The limb is a sturdy one, doesn't sway at all with his weight. He grabs another branch, above his head, and begins to climb.

"Where you headed?" Odom asks.

"See if I can knock the stump loose out of there," his son says. He is a fast climber, already halfway up to where the stump hangs. Odom's ears continue their ringing, and he has to concentrate on the movement of his son's lips to know what he's saying. The tree's branches are skinny where the son is climbing now, and they bend dangerously under his weight.

"Just leave it," Odom says.

The son takes another branch, and another, before he answers. "I'm most the way there already," he says.

"What do we want it down here for?" Odom says.

The son shakes the branches around him, bounces on the springy limb. "Next big wind will just bring it loose," he says.

"Then let the wind do it," Odom says.

The son hesitates, then slips down the trunk of the tree. He drops the last seven or eight feet to the ground, lands on the balls of his feet, straightens up quickly. He grins at Odom. "I bet one stick's worth will do for stumps from here on out," he says.

"And a further place to go," Odom says. He is blinking rapidly. His eyes smart.

Odom's son looks at him strangely, then reaches out a hand as if to stroke the side of his head, which is raw and sensitive. Odom pulls away, grasps his son's wrist. He is surprised at the thickness of the wrist, and at the strength in the arm that shakes his grip off. "Let me," the son says, and he touches the tips of his fingers to Odom's ear. He draws his hand back, and there is blood on it.

"Your ear," the son says. He holds up his hand with its darkened fingerpads, revolves it before his eyes, then wipes it carefully on his pants leg. "You got blood coming out your ear," he says to his father, looking the man square in the face. He speaks the words slowly and carefully, as though he doesn't want his father to mistake the damage that has been done.

Odom puts a plate of bacon and beans on the table in front of his son, and another at his own place. A fine gray dust layers the skin and clothes of both men. Odom's eyes are traversed with broken blood vessels, feel hot and overlarge as he pads about the kitchen. He pulls the coffeepot off a glowing stove burner, pours two cups full.

The son is already well into his food, taking up grease with a piece of bread. There is a pile of slices on a saucer set next to his place. He holds his head low over his plate.

Odom draws a forkful of beans, chews them, swallows. He hasn't got much of an appetite. The beans are already cool though he pulled them off the stove only minutes before. He and his son live in a cold house. The floor is made of poorly finished pine boards. They are fitted loosely, and the chill of the soil under the place rises from between them.

"I've decided we'll take out that locust tree tomorrow," Odom says. He has packed his injured ear with a wad of cotton batting. The ruptured eardrum aches fiercely.

The son looks up. "You sure?" he says. "We don't strictly have to. It don't lie in the way of nothing."

"I'm sure," Odom says. "We'll knock it down first thing."

The son goes back to his plate of beans. Odom takes a slice of soft bread from the saucer, swabs at his food with it. He prefers a piece of coarse grainy cornbread hot out of the pan, with a dollop of salty butter, but he hasn't recently taken the time to make any. There is no butter in the place, and hasn't been for some while.

"Locust tree draws lightning," Odom says. "More than spruce or walnut or elm. More than any other tree in the forest."

"I heard that before," his son says.

"Not the kind of a thing to have near a house," Odom says.

His son stands up from the table, sets his empty plate and his coffee cup in the sink. He runs water on them. He wets his hands too, splashes water on his face, drags his fingers back through his hair. The fingers leave damp tracks. When he straightens up from the sink he says, "Believe I'll use the truck this evening."

"You got a place you need to go?" Odom asks.

"To the valley. Some folks I want to see there."

"Sure," Odom says. "You bet."

The son retrieves the truck keys from where they hang, on a coat hook near the door. He struggles into a denim jacket with a thick fleece collar. The jacket is a couple of sizes too small for him, and it is splitting down the seam between the shoulders.

"Listen," Odom says. He gestures at the thin unpainted walls around him. "I know this ain't much. It's nothing to come home to." He leans forward, braces his arms against the edge of the table. "But that new house. When we get that built," he says, and leaves the sentence unfinished.

"It'll be quite a day," his son says.

"It will be," Odom says. "We'd of been there already, but the crawler crapped out on us."

"I know that," the son says. "I know where we'd be." He is buttoning up the jacket. He has his index finger hooked through the key ring, and the truck keys jingle in his hand.

"Better to build it by hand anyway," Odom says. His son says nothing.

"Well," Odom says. "You have yourself a good time."

"I'll do her," the son says. He leaves the house. Odom can picture him crossing the meager dirt dooryard, unchocking the trunk's front end, swinging himself into the cab as the truck starts to roll down the slope. He listens for the popping of the clutch and the rumble of the motor but hears only the new strange depthless rushing of his punctured eardrum. The truck's headlights sweep the kitchen walls, throwing slashed diagonals of light across the room in one direction as the truck backs, and then in the other as it heads off.

Odom's house is built at the edge of a steep bluff, overlooking the mountain road that leads away from his place. Odom watches from the window as the truck follows the road down, slaloming through the series of steep widening switchbacks: red taillights on one pass, dim canted headlights on the next, growing smaller and more distant with each reversal. In a few minutes the truck executes the final tight S-curve and descends altogether out of the line of his sight.

Twice now Odom has made the long walk along the roads his son might have taken when he left several nights back. He goes as far down the mountain as he can get and reasonably hope to walk back: dirt roads and gravel cutoffs and blacktop one-lane highways streaked with slick red clay. He examines gullies and crumbling embankments and hopscotches his way down wooded inclines, looking for the wrecked truck that he imagines, and the body of his son. His calves ache with the effort of descending and of climbing again.

In his searching he finds a desolate Volkswagen Beetle on its roof in a reeking sump and, further on, enmeshed in a rustling hedge of rhododendron, an elderly Nash convertible. The rhododendron has grown up through the floorboards of the car and out of the rotted cloth top. Caught in the Nash's shattered grillwork is the narrow rib cage of a deer.

Long after midnight, when he has been walking for hours, a black finned Lincoln with suicide doors rolls slowly past him, weaving down the road, left tires flirting with the cliffside

edge of the pavement. It looks to Odom as though there are
only little boys in the car, maybe half a dozen of them, the
oldest no more than about eleven. They pass him at their
sedate pace, and as they round the deep curve ahead, moving
uphill, their faces gather at the wide rear window, pale as
little moons behind the glass. They stare at him as though
they think he might be a dangerous psychopath out wandering
the roads alone.

Later, he follows the course of a dry stream that parallels the
road. There he runs across a truck that is much like his own,
and his breath catches in his throat. But this truck is a different
color from his, has been stripped of its tires and wheels and
engine long ago. The wooden stakes around the rusted
truckbed sit loose in their sockets, and the wind rattles them
as it rushes down the smooth-stoned channel.

The sheriff's deputy finds Odom in the partially cleared lot
out behind the little shanty house on the bluff. Odom is
perched in the saddle of the busted crawler, eating from a can
of cling peaches that he has opened with the short blade of
his pocketknife. His hands are dark with engine grease and
there is a smear of the stuff on his forehead. He wipes his
mouth with the back of his hand as the deputy approaches.

The deputy is a man in his middle years, dressed in loose
comfortable khaki clothes and a short military-style jacket
which is inadequate to keep him warm in the winter temperature. He has shaved carelessly, and there is a patch of light
stubble under the shelf of his jaw. He makes a gesture of
greeting at Odom. Odom fishes a yellow slice of peach from
the can and holds it out to the deputy, pinned between the

blade of the knife and his thumb. When the deputy shakes his head no, Odom slides the section into his mouth, drinks sweet juice from the can.

"You're Odom, ain't you?" the deputy asks. Odom says nothing, just looks at him. "Einer Odom," the deputy says.

Odom nods as if he has this moment recognized the name. "Yes," he says. "That's me."

"You got a boy," the deputy says. Odom has gone silent again. "A boy about seventeen." Coaxing, now.

"Yes," Odom says slowly, hesitant.

The deputy leans back, hooks his fingers in his wide gunbelt, hitches at the belt with its heavy revolver and cinch of brass cartridges. He takes a deep breath. "Look," he says, "I dealt with enough of you crazy backward ridge-running mountain rats in my lifetime." His words are measured and softly spoken, with no trace of anger in them. "I don't figure to freeze my ass out in the cold and listen to you hem and haw all day. Now why don't you tell me something about your boy."

"He went down into the valley, into town. He's been gone a few days," Odom says.

"Of course he has," the deputy says. "I got him in the county lockup. Drunk and disorderly. That your truck he's driving?"

Odom relaxes a little against the crawler's seat.

"I said, that your truck he's driving?"

Odom stirs, says, "Yes, it's my truck."

"Minus one fender," the deputy says. "He got into a scrape at a roadhouse in the levels. How much do you know about what he does when he's not here?"

Odom shrugs, wondering if that is response enough to satisfy this deputy. "Not much, I guess," he says.

"I guess," the deputy says. "He runs with a pretty rough

crowd is what he does. Drinking and starting fights. We stopped him before he did anything real bad. Anyway, he's a minor, so I come up to tell you what he's been doing. You want my advice, I'd keep him closer to home now on."

"I will," Odom says. "Surely."

"The other evening he told me a thing that I found interesting," the deputy says. "I asked him what he does up here days, and he said you and him are clearing some land for your homestead. He said you were blasting stumps. I thought maybe that was what happened to your ear there." He points to the crude head bandage Odom has fashioned out of a neckerchief.

Odom's eyes narrow. He thinks of the crate of black-market dynamite sitting in the earthen root cellar under the house, filmed in a sweat of nitroglycerine. He thinks of the carton of blasting caps with its warnings printed in fading primary colors on the rotting cardboard, and the bale of brittle fuse.

"I see he's mistaken, though," the deputy says. His voice is still cool. "I see he was confused. You're snaking them trees out of here with that 'dozer, not fooling with any damn bootleg dynamite."

Odom looks down at the crawler, which is clearly incapacitated. The offside tread is broken, has slid from the driving wheels and lies in a twisted loop behind the machine, its metal cleats clotted with mud. The blade is tilted against a granite outcropping, listing heavily to one side. The surface of the blade is carved and bent, and bright new metal shows through in half-a-dozen places where hard rock has scored the plate.

"Well," Odom says, setting the can of peaches on the bulldozer's running board and standing up, "we got a problem with the crawler at the moment."

"But you're fixing it," the deputy says, indicating the grease on Odom's hands. "It'll be all right here after a while and then you can start up again."

"Oh sure," Odom says. His voice is small. He blew the crawler's engine trying to push the half-buried granite boulder aside, just as he broke the blade and snapped the tread. He has no chainfall to pull the engine, no new engine to replace it with, no way to get one. Too tired to trek the roads anymore, he's just been fooling with it for something to do.

"That's a good thing, then," the deputy says.

"My boy," Odom says. "He'll be coming home?"

"No doubt," the deputy says. "Anyway, we're releasing him."

Odom climbs down off the crawler, stands waiting for the deputy to leave. His legs are sore from all the walking, and he wants to sit again. The deputy glances around the clearing, and his gaze fastens on something behind Odom, high over his shoulder. The hickory stump, Odom realizes, still hung up in the black locust.

"The one occasion I recall fooling with dynamite," the deputy says, and he's looking at Odom now, and not at the stump, "was the time my uncle stole a few sticks from the limestone quarry where he was working. He got his hands on some underwater fuses, too, and he took me out fishing with him."

Odom shifts from foot to foot, and the deputy peers closely at him. "I ain't boring you with this, am I?" he asks. "I wouldn't want to keep you from something you got to do."

"Oh no," Odom says.

The deputy continues. "We went out on the lake in his little rowboat, no motor or nothing. He said he would take me if I did the rowing, so I pulled us all the way out into the middle of that lake. We sat out there in the mist on that black dark water and it was like we were a million miles from the shore. Then he snapped a fuse and chucked one of the sticks of dynamite over the side of the boat.

"I was leaning over the gunwale watching when it went off, and I like to got drownded in the geyser. The water come up and slapped me in the head and lifted the rowboat and us in it, and a minute later the fishes floated to the surface, all dead from the concussion. Bass, bluegill, pike, perch, some walleye. We just scooped them into the boat by the armload. You ever seen a fish that got wasted with dynamite?"

Odom shakes his head. "No," he says. "Never have."

"Well," the deputy says, "they look like they got the surprise of their life. Mouths agape, like this." He drops his jaw in imitation. "That first bunch filled the bottom of the boat, and then he popped another stick, and a third. We like to sank, we took in that many fish.

"We got them home in his little station wagon, which never did smell the same again, and we froze a mess of them and smoked a bunch more into fish jerky on wooden racks we built out behind the house. In the end we had so many left over we had to grind them up, bones and scales and all, and plow them into my mother's garden plot for fertilizer. It stank like hell in the heat, but you should of seen them squash and sunflowers grow."

"We're planning to put us in a garden," Odom says. "It'll go on the south side of the house. I figure we'll get most of the produce we need out of it if we're lucky, and won't have to make the haul down the mountain so much."

"Sure," the deputy says. "That's a fine idea." He stretches his arms out above his head, then slaps his hands against his thighs. "It is cold up here. I swear to God, it's twenty degrees colder on this ridge than it is anywhere in the county." He turns and heads off around the shanty. Odom follows him to where he has parked his cruiser. It is a blue Mercury with bubble lights on top and a riot gun fastened upright to the dashboard.

"Tell my boy when you see him to come on back up here," Odom says. "Tell him I need him to help me with the clearing."

"If I see him," the deputy says, climbing into the cruiser. "They'll probably of turned him loose by the time I get back." He starts the car, backs and fills, backs and fills in the little turnaround Odom has cut into the hillside, and finally gets his vehicle pointed in the direction from which he came, on the road that leads to the valley floor.

Odom takes his time dropping the black locust, figures all the angles, but in the end some unexpected thing—the weight of the hickory stump trapped in its branches, or an errant gust of wind fifty feet up, or an unseen inequity in the distribution of the flesh of the tree—causes it to fall wrong, and it catches against a slim dogwood that stands across the clearing, bends the smaller tree almost double. When the locust hits, the hickory stump slips from its branches and thumps to the ground.

With his smoking, chattering chainsaw, Odom sections the locust where it has wedged, excises it neatly and expertly from the dogwood, but the little tree is badly broken. It trails its sleek limbs on the ground. Though he wanted it for a sweet-blossoming decoration in his new front yard, Odom cuts the dogwood too, and lays its slight trunk next to the locust's dark burly one.

Odom examines the stump of the locust and finds that a

groundhog has established its den, with two or three entrances, around and under the meaty roots of the tree. He won't have to sink a shaft under this stump as he did with the hickory tree. He grins, retrieves a stick of dynamite from the root cellar, with a blasting cap and a strip of fuse. He slits the damp casing of the dynamite with his knife, dumps out the innards into his hands, forms the yielding mix of nitroglycerine and sawdust into a lump the size and approximate shape of a baseball.

He reaches into the hole nearest him. The ground is frosty to a depth of about six inches; below that the dirt is soft and unfrozen. Odom inserts his arm up to the elbow, then midway to the shoulder, finds what he takes to be an appendix to the tunnel. He tucks the ball of explosive into the pocket, withdraws his arm, and crimps the soft copper blasting cap around the fuse. When he slides his arm back into the hole to insert the cap into the dynamite, his hand follows a slightly different path, down a steeply slanting fork.

He gives a grunt of surprise when he doesn't find the dynamite where he expected it, thrusts his arm in up to the shoulder. His hand is in a large open space at the arm's full extension, cool air around it rather than warm dirt, and he is surprised by the apparent size of the tunnel complex. He pulls free of the groundhog hole, slides his arm in again, searches in vain for the dynamite. He extracts his arm, licks his lips, tries once more. This time he is lucky and locates the explosive right away. He sticks the blasting cap deep into it. Then he scoops loose earth from around the mouth of the hole back into the burrow and presses it against the dynamite.

He sits near the opening, brushing dirt from his hands and regarding the fuse. He has cut a piece about a yard long, which should give him three minutes or so to get clear. Plenty of time. He pats his pockets, searching for the box of matches. When he doesn't find them, he goes back to the shanty. The matches are on the kitchen table, where his son left them. They are Ohio Blue Tip matches, the kind with the Indian head on the cover. He takes them up, returns to the locust stump.

There he lights the fuse. As it burns its laggard way into the hole, he trots away from it. He moves toward the windfall oak, then cuts away from that shelter, crosses the clearing to the granite boulder and, on the other side of it, the crawler. He climbs over both of them, pleased with his agility and the fading soreness of his muscles. He settles with his back against the crawler, on the side where the tread is whole. He presses his hands lightly to his ears, facing the house.

When the dynamite goes off, the shanty's windows ripple like water in their frames. Putty crumbles from around one or two of the panes. Odom stands, checks himself all over, laughs to find that his hands are shaking. A plume of dust and smoke stands over the blast site, already ragged and dispersing in the breeze.

Odom trots back into the clearing, scanning the nearby trees for signs of the locust stump. It is nowhere to be seen, and he is puzzled, until he finds it still in its place. It lies on its side, many of its roots still sunk in the ground. A number of them have torn loose, enough for the stump to have toppled, and the wood there is blond and new. The groundhog's tunnels have vented off the force of the blast, and the stump has only been damaged, not torn loose and thrown clear as it should have been.

Odom puts his hands on the capsized stump, which is the size of a fifty-five-gallon drum, and shoves at it. It doesn't move. He shifts his grip, tucks his shoulder under a projecting root. He throws his weight against it, but the stump is immovable. His feet piston the ground, fight for purchase, slip on the dirt. Odom stands back from the stump and stares at it for a moment, breathing hard.

"You son of a gun," he says. He kicks the stump, and the pain of the impact jars a cry from him. He leans into it, claws at it, feels one of his fingernails peel away, feels bark slipping from the hard smooth wood underneath. He flings the loosened bark into the air around him, grinds it between his palms. "You don't think you're ever coming loose out of there, do you," he says. He begins to weep, and the sound echoes off the rocks and hollows that surround him.

After a time, he sits down on the stump, growing quiet. From where he sits, he can see into the groundhog's den. The locust stump has prized up the roof of the burrow in falling, and much of the dirt, sparkling with ice crystals, remains trapped in the wide tangle of its roots. The burrow itself consists of a maze of tunnels, laid in the earth like halved clay pipes. Many of them have collapsed from the force of the blast, but a number survived. Odom is astonished by the size of the warren.

He wonders how old the groundhog is that built it, and how long it took to dig the place. Though he cannot know, he suspects that there is a layer of tunnels set below this exposed level, and another below that, and another, down through the skin of the mountain to bedrock. He imagines that there is a groundhog down below him in its smooth-walled darkness, looking up with weak piggy eyes and snuffing the air for some clue as to what cataclysm has befallen the upper world.

He imagines that after the groundhog has paused briefly in wondering, it shambles down its close corridors in the direction it was already heading, and when it comes to the end of that tunnel, it sets its shoulder against the dense earth face, and its claws, and its teeth, and simply digs and digs and digs.

Odom sits on his haunches in the root cellar. The long coat he wears is rimed with frost. Sleet clatters against the cellar door, which is set into the ground at a slant, propped open now for light. The clay walls of the cellar are hung with thin sheets of crackling ice. Odom draws his shoulders in toward his neck. He is counting the sticks of dynamite that are left in the crate, toting them up in his head against the land he wants to clear. His lips move as he calculates, but he says nothing. When he counts a stick, he moves it delicately from one side of the crate to the other.

When he is finished with the dynamite, he moves on to the box of blasting caps. He takes up a handful of the pencil-width sticks, and another, stops when he is satisfied that he has enough. He measures off an arm's length of fuse, which is stiff from the cold, and cuts it with his pocketknife. His hands are grimy with ash, and they tremble. He stuffs the fuse into one of the long side pockets of his coat, drops in a couple of blasting caps after it.

He takes up a stick of the dynamite, two. He stands a moment, considering. Then he takes up a third stick and quickly climbs the steep wooden stairs that lead up from the cellar. A rotten stair tread gives under his weight, and he stumbles, catching himself with one hand, clutching the dynamite to his breast with the other. He clucks his displeasure at himself, then rises.

Out in the slaty daylight, he swings the heavy door to and

snaps shut the padlock that secures it. He straightens his coat around his legs, turns the collar up with his free hand, and heads off toward the clearing.

Odom's son switches off the truck, hops out, chocks the wheels before it can get away from him down the grade. The truck's crumpled right fender is fastened to the body with a twist of heavy-gauge baling wire. The son looks at the gray weathered shanty and the woods around but does not see his father. Then a sound comes to him from the clearing behind the house: an arrhythmic tolling, metal on metal; twice; three times; then it ceases.

"Hey," he calls. "I'm back." He leans into the truck cab, gathers a couple of grocery bags into his arms, pushes the door shut with his hip. The hammering sound starts up again. He pauses near the bed of the truck, where there are two battered canisters of LP gas, but decides to leave them where they are until later.

He enters the house, sets the bags down in the frigid kitchen. His breath mists when he exhales. He puts his hand on the propane heater in the corner and finds it cold. He shakes his head, goes to the window. When he looks out, he sees his father hunched against the granite outcropping, wielding a small claw hammer. He swings it clumsily, his grip high, just under the hammer's head. When the hammer comes down, metal chimes.

The son's eyes widen when he looks beyond Odom and the boulder to the clearing. The ground there is torn and pitted, as though an artillery barrage has walked through it. A large number of trees are gone. They have evidently been cut and sectioned, their branches sliced away and piled together for a coming bonfire, the stumps blown and removed. Those are the trees closest to the shanty.

Farther away, the trees are down, but they have not been cut. They have been blasted wholesale from the ground, and the seared trunks lie at startling removes from the tangles of their roots. The trees are tumbled pell-mell over one another, two and even three deep, in a welter of sap and pith and broken wood. Odom has cleared enough space for a mansion, for the home of a giant.

The son leaves the shanty and goes to Odom, who is still flailing at the rock. He grips a short stone drill in his left hand, strikes it with the hammer, turns the bit, strikes it again. As the son watches, the head of Odom's hammer misses the drill, grazes his fingers, bounces off the boulder. A spray of broken rock flies up, and Odom turns his head aside to avoid it. He pulls the bit from the rock, drops it, sucks at his bruised fingers.

"Hey Poppy," the son says. His voice is quiet. "I come back." He has been gone for nine days. Odom has lost weight in his son's absence. His gabardines hang on him. There are dark crescents under his eyes, smears of sleeplessness like lampblack. The light hammer hangs at his side. When he bends to set it down, his son sees that the skin and hair on one side of his head have been crisped. The son catches briefly the scent of a burn.

"What happened to your head?" he asks.

Odom raises his right hand absently to the hurt place and touches it lightly, as though to familiarize himself with his changed profile. "Oh yeah," he says, and his voice is unnaturally loud in the stillness on the ridge. "Fire jumped right down the fuse a couple days back. Got a premature blast, and I didn't have time but to skip away a little."

The hand that scrapes at Odom's skull is wrapped in a stained bandanna. Because the hand is in continual motion, Odom's son cannot tell if there is a full complement of fingers inside the bandage. The nails of the fingers that he can make out are blackened and split. Odom turns away to look toward the clearing. "You see what I done?" he says.

"I seen," the son says, but Odom doesn't turn back to him or respond.

"I knocked them down," Odom says, gesturing at the cascade of flattened trees. "Now all we got to do is shift them trunks out of there, break up this rock, and we can lay the foundation. We'll be in by spring." He turns back to his son, stares at him. His bloodshot eyes are tearing, and he wipes at them with the back of his hand. "You see?" he says.

"I see," the son says. Odom nods enthusiastically.

"You should," he says. "You should see, when I light off a charge under a big pine tree. Sucker rides the blast up and up, just like a rocket, up into the sky. Branches flatten against the trunk. Then it turns and slides and falls back. Can't always tell where it's going to fall, though," he says, and his tone sounds as though it is born of regret, "so you got to keep a sharp eye out. Stay on your toes."

The son begins to reply, but Odom pushes past him, circles the boulder to where the crawler sits, returns with a four-pound sledgehammer and a long star drill cradled against his chest. He presses the hammer on his son, who holds the rough wooden haft of it, resting the rectangular head in the dirt at his feet.

"But now," Odom says, "you're back, and we can make some real progress."

"I brought some food up with me," the son says, but Odom has turned from him again. "I got canned goods."

"That was the simple part," Odom says. He swings his wounded hand out toward the trees, and the gesture is dismissive. He pats the side of the boulder, almost with affection. He fingers the hole he has begun in its side. "Now this," he says, "this here is the real bitch-kitty."

"I brought up some propane," the son says, and now his voice is almost pleading. He drops the handle of the hammer. Odom notices, stoops to pick it up, hands it once more to his son. "For the stove, and the heaters," the son says. He tries not to stare at his father's slightened figure. "Let's get you something to eat."

Odom inspects the cutting edge of the star drill, slips it into the hole in the granite. While he holds the long bit clumsily in both hands, he says to his son, "Go ahead on. I can't swing the hammer good, so I'll turn the bit."

The son raises the hammer, lowers it again. "I don't," he says. "I don't believe I can."

"Go to it," Odom says. "Faster you cut the hole, faster we can set the charge and blow this son of a gun."

The son cocks the hammer, makes a tentative pass with it at the end of the drill bit. The hammer's head clinks against it, skitters off, barely misses Odom. He doesn't flinch. "That's it," he says, and turns the bit in the hole. "Now get some fire into it."

"I'll mash your hands," the son says, but already he has the hammer in motion. It describes a brief arc through the air, strikes the bit, makes the metal clang and hum. The handle of the hammer vibrates, stings the palms of his hands. Rock dust puffs out of the hole.

"Go," Odom says, and he turns the bit again. The son brings the hammer over his shoulder, connects. Odom twists the drill. The son swings again.

"This is how they built the railroads," Odom says. He pauses to turn the drill, which is growing warm. It buzzes as though it might be alive with electricity. "They cut a hole in the rockbed by hand, then dropped the charge in." The son misses a stroke, stumbles forward. He moves back to his place, looks at his father, but Odom is concentrating on the quivering bit in his hands.

"They had a guy that sang to keep them in time," Odom says. The son strikes the drill bit solidly. "That way they never missed a beat," Odom says. Then he begins to sing.

The son stands and listens for a moment. He cannot recall ever having heard his father sing before. "Drill ye tarriers, drill," Odom sings. His voice is hard and tuneless. The son brings the hammer smartly down on the drill. He is surprised to see that the bit sinks appreciably with every blow.

"And blast, and fire," Odom sings. Soon the son finds the rhythm of the song, ignores the abrasions the hammer provokes on the skin of his palms. "And it's work all day for sugar in your tay," Odom bellows, "down behind the railway." The son finds that he is more accurate if he doesn't look at the wavering end of the bit but watches instead the blistered side of his father's head.

For his part, Odom keeps his eyes on the steadily deepening hole in the rock, singing at the top of his lungs, the vapor of his breath condensing and swirling around him in the cold. "Drill ye tarriers, drill," he sings, beginning again, and the son cannot tell whether it is the second time he has heard the verse, or the third, or the hundredth. He continues to heft the hammer. Each time its heavy head rings against the drill, Odom gives the bit a quarter turn. And joined together in that slow mechanical labor, the two men drive a narrow shaft toward the hidden bitter heart of the rock.

ABOUT THE AUTHOR

Pinckney Benedict was born in 1964. He grew up and continues to live on his family's dairy farm, not far north of Lewisburg, West Virginia. He holds a bachelor's degree from Princeton University, where he studied creative writing with Joyce Carol Oates, and a master's degree from the creative writing program of the University of Iowa. His first collection of short stories, *Town Smokes*, was published in 1987 to wide acclaim; included in that collection was "The Sutton Pie Safe," for which Mr. Benedict received the Nelson Algren Award, given by the *Chicago Tribune*. He has also received a James Michener Fellowship from the Writers' Workshop. He is currently at work on a novel.